Love & Joy

Holidays in Hallbrook

Elsie Davis

Sweet Romance Publishing

Sweet Romance Publishing

Sweetromancepublishing.com

PO Box 778

Liberty, NC 27298

Many thanks to all my readers who have loved the Holiday in Hallbrook series.
It's your reviews and enthusiasm that me writing more! Hugs!!

James 1:6
But when you ask, you must believe and not doubt,
because the one who doubts is like a wave of the sea, blown and tossed by the wind.

Chapter One

♥

I T HAD BEEN A long and busy day for Zoe at Peterson's Ice Creamery. As an assistant manager, the tasks of manager fell gently on her shoulders since the shop didn't have one. Never had one for that matter. It was a situation she was trying to rectify, but one that always seemed just out of reach.

Zoe drove to the Parker residence to pick her son up, preparing herself for the inevitable battle ahead. She was sure it would be the same old *I don't want to go home yet* routine, Scott much preferring to stay and play with Devon, his best friend. She was grateful, however, that Iris Parker was willing to watch the boys after school. She claimed it was easier to keep up with her grandson when Scott was around. Whatever her reasons, it also made Zoe's life easier. All except the picking up part. Just this one time, it would be nice if he was ready and willing to leave.

Not only had Old Man Peterson not come through yet with an offer for her promotion to manager, but it was her thirtieth birthday, and no one remembered. No one had offered her birthday wishes at the shop. And no one had called, well, all except her mother, that is. Not even Sarah Peterson, her best friend, had called yet. She shouldn't let it get to her, but the truth was, it hurt.

If it hadn't been for her mother's phone call, Zoe might have thought she got the date wrong and that today wasn't March eighth. She was tempted to call Sarah if only to see whether the sound of her voice jogged her friend's memory. The problem was Sarah had a new boyfriend, which meant she had love on the brain. Lately, Dalton saw more of Sarah than Zoe did. Not that she begrudged her friend a loving relationship.

It's just that today should have been special. Instead, a night of television and romances that made her cry on the Hallmark channel would be her party. Scott hadn't remembered this morning before she dropped him off at school, but then he was only nine years old. And as to everyone else, Zoe wasn't the kind of person who would remind them.

Life certainly wasn't turning out the way she expected. She'd worked at the creamery since she was sixteen, except for a couple of years when she went away to school. It was then she'd fallen in love, got married, became a mother, and then returned home divorced and with her tail between her legs. A single-mother role had not been in her plans.

Back in Hallbrook, Mack Peterson had hired her at once, and a few years ago, had promoted her to assistant manager. When Old Man Peterson let her know he'd been thinking of filling the position of manager, she'd been all for it, hoping he'd choose her. She was the most-likely candidate considering her years of experience there, but so far, there was no word. It was as if he'd forgotten he ever mentioned it to her.

At thirty, she needed more from life.

She turned down Blue Spruce Lane and into the Parker's driveway. Luckily, it hadn't snowed this past week and there were only small patches of ice scattered across the surface where the salt hadn't reached. It had been a mild winter in New Hampshire, something Zoe didn't mind at all as it was her least favorite season of the year.

Turning off the engine, she started to get out of the car as a flurry of activity ensued on the front porch. Scott and Devon stood there, her son dressed in his winter coat, hat, and boots.

"Hi, Mom. I'm ready to go," Scott said, stepping off the porch.

Thank you for this small miracle, Lord.

"Hi, Ms. Carruthers," Devon called out from where he stood next to Scott, dressed only in jeans, a sweater, and sneakers. They clearly hadn't been out playing, which made this an even bigger miracle—a birthday present of sorts.

"Hey, boys. Did you have a good day at school? Is everything okay?" she asked, looking back and forth between them, hoping they weren't fussing with one another. Scott would be sullen all evening if that were the case.

"School was okay. You know, regular stuff. Boring." Scott shrugged, turning back to Devon. "See you tonight."

His friend glared at him.

Zoe didn't know of any plans Scott might have made, especially considering she'd hoped tonight would be something special with Sarah. A dinner out at O'Malley's would have been nice, but it would seem even that wasn't destined to happen.

"I meant tomorrow," Scott corrected, waving to his friend as he got in the car.

Zoe frowned, wondering what the two were up to. They were acting weird, and when kids and weird happened in the same sentence, there was usually trouble. "Where's your grandmother?"

"She's on the phone with someone," Devon said quickly—almost too quickly.

"Okay. Can you tell her I was here and picked Scott up, so she won't worry when she notices him missing?"

Devon jumped up and down on the porch, his arms wrapped around his chest. "I will. I'm freezing out here. Bye," he said, turning and running back into the house without waiting for an answer.

Zoe slid back in the car, started it, and cranked up the heater. She put the car in reverse and backed down the driveway. "So, what was that all about with Devon? The whole tonight thing," she clarified. A quick glance in his direction told her she'd caught him off guard. There was definitely something up between the two of them and it was her job as a parent to figure it out and dig deeper.

"Nothing. I'm not supposed to say," Scott mumbled, turning his head to look out the window.

"We don't keep secrets, young man. You know the rules." For years, she'd tried to make sure they were close enough he'd trust her enough to keep her informed, knowing it was the easiest way to keep him safe. She was forced to play the roles of both mom and dad, and she took the roles very seriously.

"I know, but...fine. Devon wants me to hang with him tonight, but he hasn't asked his parents, so I'm not supposed to say anything yet."

"But why is that a problem?"

"I don't know. He's weird like that, I guess. Something about asking first before planning stuff so they don't feel bad saying no. Sounds dumb to me, but that's one of their rules." Scott shrugged and leaned forward to turn on the radio.

"Sounds like a good rule to me. It does put people on the spot if they need to say no. Where were you planning to go? And is it something you really want to do?" Zoe prayed he'd say no. A birthday celebration by herself would be totally lame. She'd counted on having Scott around at the very least.

"The Peterson's skating rink. And yes, I like hanging out over there." Her son turned a smiling face toward her, his eyes lit with animation. "There's always lots of kids from school."

"I see. Well, it's fine by me if they call. Why don't we wait and see what happens?" She wouldn't stop him from going for her own selfish reasons even if the thought of spending the night home alone was depressing.

"Thanks, Mom. Sounds good." Scott nodded. He turned to look out the window and was silent the rest of the way home.

Back at the house, Zoe hung up her jacket, while Scott flung his on the couch and raced down the hall.

"Scott, hang up your jacket," she hollered, but it was too late; the kid was long gone. She let out a deep breath. Moving to the fireplace, she tossed in three logs and a starter brick, hoping a fire would take off some of the chill.

Dinner was next on the agenda, and she headed for the kitchen after hanging up her son's coat. It was easier than making him do it, and tonight, she wasn't up for the battle. Taking the spaghetti sauce that she'd made this past weekend out of the refrigerator, she dumped it in a pan and turned the stove on low. Putting water in another pan for the spaghetti, she placed it next to the sauce and turned the heat on high to bring it to a boil.

Her cell phone rang. Finally. Someone, hopefully, Sarah, was calling to wish her a happy birthday.

Zoe picked up the phone, glancing at the screen, a half-smile on her face. One that turned into a half-frown when she saw Leslie Parker's name. Devon's mother would only be calling for one thing. She'd said yes to the rink, and now the decision was on Zoe to agree or play the bad guy and say no. Having already told Scott yes, she wouldn't change her mind. She answered the call on the third ring. "Hey, Leslie."

"Hi, Zoe. I'm not bothering you, am I?" Devon's mother was always nice and the two of them got along well, although they didn't run in the same circles. Leslie was in the happily-married-with-children circle.

"No, I just started to fix dinner. What's up?" she asked, not wanting to let on that she already knew the reason for the call. It wouldn't do to get Devon in trouble over something like this.

"I know it's last minute and all, but Devon wants Scott to go skating tonight. Would that be all right with you?"

"Absolutely." *Not.* So much for watching movies curled up with her son. She'd be flying solo tonight. Although to be fair, Hallmark movies weren't Scott's idea of fun. He preferred superhero movies. "What time?"

"Let's say in thirty minutes. If you drop him off at the rink, I'll see to it they get something to eat from the hot dog stand. I'll bring Scott home around nine if that's okay with you."

"Let me double-check with Scott really quick to make sure his homework is done." Mondays were always heavy homework days, the teachers taking advantage of fresh brains after the weekend. She also wanted to make sure her son hadn't changed his mind, or better still, remembered her birthday and would opt to stay home.

Zoe muted the phone and headed down the hall. She opened Scott's bedroom door and poked her head into the room. "Mrs. Peterson's on the phone. Do you want to go skating?" Zoe asked, silently hoping he'd say no.

"Cool. I'm ready," he said. He'd already changed his clothes and put on a nice shirt for the event. It made her wonder if there was a girl he was trying to impress. He was growing up fast.

"Finish your homework yet?" she asked, always in mom mode.

"Don't have any." Scott beamed. "Can I go now?"

"His mother plans to be at the rink in thirty minutes. So, cool your skates, young man," she teased. Zoe unmuted the phone. "It's a go, of course. See you there."

"Perfect. Talk to you soon," Leslie said before hanging up.

"She's going to get you dinner at the rink, so I'll go turn off the spaghetti until I get back."

"Yum, I love the corn dogs and fries," he said, rubbing his belly.

"Try to eat just one corn dog, please. I don't need you home with a bellyache tomorrow." It wasn't the healthiest of meals, but then life deserved treats now and then. In fact, Zoe decided, tonight might be the perfect night to treat herself. A quick stop by The Sweeter Side of Life after dropping Scott off, and she'd pick up a dozen donuts for her dessert. Not that she'd eat them all, but a couple during the movie wouldn't hurt.

"I don't see the Parker's car here yet and we're a little early," Zoe said, making a final drive down the last row of cars. She pulled into a parking spot and shut off the engine. It got dark early this time of year. She picked up her purse off the front seat and swung it over her shoulder, unwilling to let Scott walk to the barn alone. "Grab your skates and I'll take you inside where you can put them on while we wait for Devon and his mom."

"Okay. I'm sure they'll be here," Scott said, looking around as they made their way to the barn.

"It would seem a lot of other folks had the same idea as you and Devon. The place is packed. Come on, let's get you inside. I don't know about you, but I'm cold out here." Puffs of frosty air meeting warm air billowed in front of her as she spoke.

Zoe looked over at the rink, noting plenty of skaters were already on the ice. Perhaps she should have asked to join the boys. Anything other than sitting at home to pout about an uneventful thirtieth birthday. She pulled the barn door open and stepped inside.

"Surprise," an entire room full of people hollered. Party horns blasted. She couldn't believe it. Friends from all directions surged forward to greet her with happy, smiling faces. Caught off guard, she laughed and hugged the well-wishers who approached.

They hadn't forgotten. Tears of joy slid down her face unchecked.

Sarah stepped forward from the crowd and hugged her. "Happy birthday, bestie." Grinning from ear to ear, her friend knew she'd pulled a good one on Zoe.

"This is all you, I'm sure. And here I thought you and everyone else forgot," Zoe said, shaking her head, still trying to take it all in.

Sarah laughed. "Are you kidding? Our silence should have been your first clue."

Zoe turned to Scott. "Did you know about this?"

His broad smile was answer enough. "Of course. Devon and I and the Parkers worked out how to get you here. I almost goofed it up, but I was quick on my feet." He nodded, high fiving Devon.

"You stinkers." The music started, and people made their way to the wooden floor set up in the center of the room and began to dance, getting into the spirit of fun. She turned to Sarah. "I still can't believe this. You tricked me good this year. I figured you were too busy with Dalton to think about me."

"No way. And he's around here somewhere. There's plenty of soft drinks and water for the kids, champagne for the adults, and food for everyone. Make sure you get something to eat and drink. I'll let you talk to some of the others while I go claim a dance from my beau." Sarah hugged her again. "I'm tickled you never found out. I always love it when I can one-up someone for their own good."

"You definitely managed that this time. I should have known you wouldn't forget. Thank you so much. This is incredible."

Sarah moved off to find her boyfriend, leaving Zoe standing there to check out all the people who had shown up for her party.

All the employees from the ice cream shop, people she knew in town, people she'd gone to school with. Sarah had invited just about everyone Zoe knew by the looks of it. She looked for Scott, but he had already left her side, the fun and excitement of a party more appealing than his mom talking to her best friend.

"Happy birthday. Can I have this dance?" a deep voice said from behind her, the man leaning close enough that his breath tickled her ear. She spun around to see who was doing the asking.

Blake Peterson.

She'd recognize Sarah's brother anywhere. Tall, sandy blond hair, and the bluest of blue eyes she'd never gotten out of her head. Not that he knew that. Two years older and popular in school, he hadn't known she existed. Well, other than when she showed up with Sarah and he was forced to talk to her—like when she and Sarah had graduated from high school.

She looked around, not wanting to misunderstand who he was talking to and look like a fool. Except there was no one else close by and it was her birthday. "Ummm...thanks. Yes, I guess," she mumbled, unsure how to answer.

Zoe didn't want to be rude, but she also didn't want to step on his feet or any number of other things she might do to make a fool of herself. Dancing with her high school crush had been something she'd dreamed of for years. At least until she left for college and married Larry. Big mistake, but he had cured her of crushing on Blake.

"*I guess* isn't very flattering," he said dryly. "Let's stick with a simple yes." His warm smile sent shivers down her spine. Maybe she wasn't as over him as she once thought—not that it mattered. This guy was so out of her league it wasn't funny, not to mention awkward, since he was Sarah's brother.

Blake led her to the dance floor just as a slow song started to play. She swallowed hard, the lump in her throat making it hard to breathe. She pulled back slightly, giving him the chance to change his mind. Taking her in his arms, Zoe put her hands on his shoulders, keeping their bodies a starchy distance apart.

"I don't bite." He laughed, drawing her in closer. Awkwardly, she slid her hands around his neck. It was a bit friendly—but it was Blake Peterson. And it was her birthday. This was the best birthday present ever.

Zoe tried to relax, letting Blake lead her around the floor. "You're a good dancer," she said, trying to think of something to say.

"Thank you. And you've grown into quite a beautiful woman," he murmured into her ear, his warm breath sending another wave of delightful shivers down her spine.

"Are you cold?" he asked, grinning down at her. Dressed in a thick sweater and the place plenty warm, he already knew she wasn't cold.

Why couldn't she be cool as a cucumber and flirt right back with the man? Because he was Blake, that's why. Flirting with him would be disastrous, and she would come up the loser. She may not have seen him around for years, but Sarah was full of stories. Blake was popular with the ladies. "I'm fine." It was the truth.

The song ended, and Blake led her to the side of the room, off to one corner. Placing one finger under her chin, he tilted her head back, gazing into her eyes. In those seconds, the rest of the room disappeared.

Why did it look as though he wanted to kiss her? He wouldn't.

His mouth landed on hers. *He did.*

Oh my.

Zoe couldn't help but respond, the mood of the party and her joy taking over and leading the way. Blake's hand cupped her face gently. It was all so romantic and magical. Perfect.

Surreal.

The truth hit Zoe over the head, and she stepped back, her hand touching her lips. "What was that for?"

"It was a birthday kiss, of course." Blake grinned, looking a little off-kilter himself.

She had to fix this and go with the flow. The fun of it. She had to be bold. "If that was a birthday kiss, I can't help but wonder what you'd do for an encore?" *Ugh.* That came out all wrong. It was as though she was asking for more kisses—which was as far from the truth as possible.

"Dance with me again and find out," he said, his eyes twinkling with merriment.

She shook her head. "That's probably not a good idea."

"Why not?" he asked, his smile slipping.

"Because you're Blake Peterson, heir to the Peterson empire, and I work for your company. I'm up for a promotion and it wouldn't look good at all to be fraternizing with you. One dance, one birthday kiss. More than enough to set the wagging tongues in this town into action. Two of either one would be more like a kiss of death—to my promotion." Zoe stepped away, putting some distance between them to reinforce her point.

She glanced around the room, hoping no one had noticed—especially Scott. Her son was protective, and the last thing she wanted to do was have him worry about her getting involved with someone. Zoe spotted him across the room with Devon, his gaze fixated on her.

Uh-oh...

Chapter Two

♥

BLAKE GRINNED AT THE curvy, blonde birthday girl. She was far too serious in her fatalistic prediction after such an interesting kiss. Little Zoe Andrews had grown into a beauty, or to be technically correct, Zoe Carruthers. "Did you learn that in acting school? The dramatic bit." He wondered about her sudden wariness, unsure of what changed, preferring the fun that came with the bolder version.

"If you actually still lived in Hallbrook, you'd realize it's not drama, but in fact, the truth," she said, still not bothering to look at him. Her unease had become more tense and distant, and far too serious.

Blake shook his head. "It was a dance, not a date," he said, grinning. "And the people in town know me and know that I'm not a matrimonial type of guy. I'm here to work, trust me. I'm back at my grandfather's special request and looking forward to digging in and trying to take Peterson Corporation to a new technological era."

"All the more reason we shouldn't have a second dance or kiss." Zoe looked back at him, an odd expression on her face.

Sarah had mentioned Zoe going off to college, a marriage, a son, and a subsequent divorce a few short years later, and then her eventual return to Hallbrook. The few times he'd come home, he hadn't seen much of her or noticed. At least, not the way he had in high school. Usually, when he visited, which wasn't often, it was with his most recent socialite on his arm. Someone to keep his attention off the boredom he associated with small-town life.

But from the moment Zoe had walked into the barn, there was no *not* noticing her. The kiss had been meant as a birthday peck, not the lip fest they both ended up enjoying. Her response and uneasiness afterward had been refreshing.

Except now.

Blake would give anything to know what she was thinking, but she seemed immune to his charm and easy-going attitude. Women normally liked having fun around him, even if he lost interest quickly. "I'm sorry about the extended kiss if that's what's bothering you."

"Who said it's bothering me?" she asked, shrugging, keeping her voice neutral.

He wasn't buying into her nonchalance. "I can tell you're upset about something, and I'm just hoping it's not me. The kiss was just a kiss between two consenting adults. A special birthday kiss, if you will." For some reason, he found that important for her to know.

"I get it. It meant nothing to you. Please drop the subject. It meant nothing to me either, if that's what's *bothering you*," she said, a forced smile on her face.

Her edginess had increased, causing him to advance rather than retreat. He was more than a little intrigued what was going on behind her sheltered expression. "Okay then, now that we've established neither one of us is interested romantically in the other person, will you save me another dance?" Blake wasn't used to this kind of interchange with a woman—the one where you had to convince them to dance or go to dinner.

"Not in this lifetime, Don Juan." Zoe walked away without so much as a backward glance.

Blake was stunned. At first, anyway. And then he remembered the kiss. There was no denying the spark he'd felt. Something he hadn't experienced in a long time—if ever. Later, he'd have to give it some thought about why. He glanced around the room and then made his way to the bar.

"I saw that big brother," Sarah said, coming to stand next to him. "She's off-limits, and that was no birthday kiss. You better not try and add her to your long, never-ending list of arm candy," she huffed, glaring at him, hands on her hips.

"I wouldn't dream of it. She's not my type." Being warned off by his sister only added to the already frustrating moment with Zoe.

"Exactly. Your type are progressive women dressed in high society clothes that want to be escorted to all the posh parties escorted by the wealthy son, high tech guru of Modern Designs, Inc. Zoe is country and blushes and sweet, and prefers jeans and a t-shirt," Sarah rattled off. "And she's my friend."

"I heard you the first time. Loud and clear. I wasn't hitting on her, and contrary to what you believe, it was just a birthday kiss." *Liar.* But until he understood his own reaction, he wasn't about to discuss it with his sister. The last thing he wanted was for her to go running back to Zoe, telling tales that would make him look the fool.

"You didn't see your best friend with stars in her eyes after the kiss. Just be careful. Good to have you home. How long are you staying?" Sarah asked switching gears.

He'd seen the light in Zoe's eyes but preferred to believe it as birthday excitement. Sarah was wrong. What kind of a girl would get stars in her eyes from just one kiss? *The Zoe kind of girl.* Sweet as Sally Little's homemade peach pie. "Is that your way of warning me off and tell me to go back to the city?"

"Maybe." She shrugged. "I don't want her to get hurt. She's been through enough with you making things worse." Blake liked that Sarah was super protective of her friend. It would be a good feeling to know someone truly had your back.

"I'm only here long enough to show Grandpa some ideas I've got regarding forward progress with the corporation. I'm hoping he's finally willing to listen and let me make some changes. With Dad at the helm, the company hasn't moved forward in twenty years."

"You two need to agree to disagree. You're still family." Sarah shook her head, frustrated with the way things stood between him and Robert Peterson. Heir to the Peterson Corporation and a stick in the mud kind of guy. *His father.*

"Sure thing, but family listens to each other, and he still acts like I'm wet behind the ears. No reason to stick around and get berated for what others consider necessary progress." It had been the same old argument between them for years and the reason he'd left Hallbrook, taking a job in New York City. Technically, it had started when he was a kid, and he'd been fed up with working on the farm the old school way.

Blake rubbed at his arm, as if thinking of the scar made it burn. Old Nellie hadn't liked him milking her much, and he'd felt the same way for the cow and the smelly, hard chores that came with a farm.

"But ultra-modern doesn't really fit the country farm image, does it? I'm sort of with Dad on this one." Nothing Blake didn't already know. Sarah and Dad had always been close. *Daddy's little girl.*

"That's because you were the girl and got all the easy chores growing up, while I was stuck with the hardest, nastiest, smelliest—"

"I get the picture, and you have a point, just not one that's going to change the way Dad sees things. You both have moved on and now you both need to let it go."

"If only it were that easy. His lectures haven't changed one bit. Tell me this—if you can design technology to cover the menial parts, making it easier, faster, cheaper...isn't that a good thing? The point of running a business is to make a profit." Streamlining was the name of Blake's game, and he was good at it. Just not for his own family's business. The problem was, he wanted to be accepted and help in the way he knew best. *Progress.*

"Yes. But what about a compromise? A middle ground you can both accept. Dad just wants to keep the town and the people who work for him happy and employed. Not let machines run them out of work and on welfare," Sarah said, sounding just like his father.

"Progress can bring in new jobs. It doesn't have to take them away, and I've got the numbers to prove it." It was like the merry-go-round of all conversations in his family.

Sarah touched his arm. "I'm glad you're here. Even if it's temporary. Who knows, maybe Dad will hear you out one day."

Blake shook his head and smiled. "It's Grandpa who asked me to come back and the one who wants to hear my ideas. Go figure."

"Nice. Straight to the top." Sarah grinned before walking away and leaving him to think about what she said. The part about Zoe, not about his dad.

Zoe stopped at the food table, helping herself to the wide array of dishes Sarah had catered in. All her favorites, from macaroni and cheese to chicken cordon bleu, and of course, cake. The German chocolate cake was monstrous, the top-loaded with thirty candles.

She glanced Scott's way again, determined they should discuss what he saw. Or, more to the point, find out how much he saw first, and then deal with it from there. Zoe started his way, but Sarah grabbed her by the arm.

"Hey, birthday girl, time for cake," she said, pulling Zoe back toward the table. Talking with Scott would have to wait.

"If I can get everyone's attention for a moment," Sarah called out loudly. The band stopped playing. "It's time to cut the cake, so if you would all gather round to sing, it would be greatly appreciated."

Zoe blushed red, the warmth lighting her face on fire.

People closed in on them, and the band started to play as they all sang "Happy Birthday" to her. Amidst cheers and clapping, Zoe leaned toward the cake and gave it her best shot to blow out the candles someone had lit during the song. She got it down to all but one.

"Looks like someone's got a boyfriend or has one coming her way," Sarah teased. The old joke was more embarrassing when you left two or more candles burning. Then it was said you had multiple boyfriends. Although, at this point, nothing could be further from the truth. There wasn't even one and hadn't been in a long time.

"Ha-ha, very funny. Too busy for that nonsense, and you know it. I'll let you have all the fun." Zoe pulled Sarah in for a hug.

Sarah cut the cake and served it up to the long line of people who waited patiently for the chocolate perfection that surely came from The Sweeter Side of Life bakery. Amanda's creations were out of this world. Luckily, Zoe got the first piece and wouldn't have to wait.

She moved to sit down at a table, first to eat her dinner, and then to savor her dessert. It was the first she'd sat down since arriving. Sarah had gone to great lengths to surprise her and had succeeded. Blake's surprise kiss, however, managed to shock her the most.

Reflecting on it now still had the ability to give her a warm, fuzzy feeling. The birthday part of the kiss was good. It was what came after the peck and before she broke it off, wherein lay the problem. The time between birthday fun and the reality that it was Blake doing the kissing.

And the kiss was way better than anything she'd dreamed about all the times she thought about what it would be like when she was in high school. *The best kiss of her life.*

Blake had asked her to dance again, and she'd run scared. Partly because of Scott, mostly because she was afraid that she might fall in love with him far too easily, and then he'd be gone, leaving her with a broken heart to mend.

It had hurt when Larry left, or perhaps it was more of an embarrassment. Scott was the one who hurt the most, but as for Zoe, not dealing with her husband's whining and complaining and late party nights was a blessing. Larry was the one who finally broke her crush on Blake, so who would help her recover from the inevitable heartbreak this time around?

Zoe glanced around the room, unable to keep from searching for Blake's handsome face. He was nowhere to be seen. She considered asking Sarah where he'd gone, but that would be tipping her hand and showing interest, something best left undone.

At least it answered her question about a second dance. There wouldn't be one whether she agreed or not. Blake had left the party.

Chapter Three

♥

TWO DAYS AFTER THE party, Zoe still couldn't get the kiss out of her head.

Back at work, life returned to the same busy schedule, the one where she filled all the roles of assistant manager and manager. At least everything except the most important decisions— like hiring, promoting, giving raises, and legal stuff. She'd sort of fallen into the role of a dual job without the title after she'd stepped up and simply started handling things around the ice cream shop that needed doing. Things that didn't require a fancy business administration degree to figure out. Old Man Peterson hadn't objected in the slightest, but then why would he? One and a half employees for the price of one.

This is why when he'd first approached her several weeks ago about a potential promotion to the manager's position, she'd been thrilled. She had fine-tuned her resume, updating it with everything she took care of at the creamery, sent it to the corporate human resources email address, and copied Mack Peterson. With her thirtieth birthday just around the corner, she'd begun to believe the job was meant to be hers. But the birthday came and went, and it hadn't happened.

Three weeks was more than enough to decide the way she saw it.

Zoe fired up the computer to check on orders and deliveries, and of course, her email. Just in case. The red flashing dot of a high priority email caught her attention. The sender was none other than Old Man Peterson himself. She grinned, a thrill of excitement racing through her. This could be it. She took a deep breath and clicked.

Dear Ms. Zoe Carruthers,

I've reviewed your resume and, of course, your employee file, and find you to be an excellent candidate for the manager's position at Peterson's Ice Creamery. Your dedication to the com-

pany is highly appreciated. Therefore, it is with great pleasure I'd like to discuss the next step toward you securing the promotion. I would like to meet with you at two o'clock today at the shop if that's an opportune time for you.

Sincerely,

Mack Peterson, CEO Peterson's Corporation

He wanted to talk to her...today. Joy rippled through her, the anticipation of success within reach. Finally, the job title and a pay raise, something she and Scott desperately needed to help ease her financial worries. Child support and her income simply weren't enough to cover the bases and be able to enjoy some of the simple things in life—like a vacation. Something long overdue but simply not affordable.

Zoe glanced at her watch. 9:15. Three hours and forty-five long minutes until she knew what he had in mind, and if, in fact, he was promoting her. She'd learned long ago not to count the proverbial chickens before they hatched, but in this case, how could she not start dreaming? *Great pleasure...discuss the next step...promotion.* It all added up to one thing—he was giving her the job. She hit reply and tried to collect her thoughts to respond.

Dear Mr. Peterson,

I look forward to meeting with you at two p.m. to discuss my future with the company. Thank you for your kind words and confidence in my abilities.

Sincerely,

Zoe Carruthers

She hit send, stood, and couldn't keep from doing a little happy dance before she settled back into the real world of orders and deliveries. Not that she achieved much, her focus non-existent. Frequent glances at the clock revealed the hands of time moving far too slowly in her opinion. Things were easier when she was working out front with the mid-day rush of customers. Old Man Peterson had timed the meeting to fall between the lunch and after-school rushes. Smart man.

The overhead bell jingled, announcing a new arrival just as Zoe removed her apron, ready to freshen up in back before the appointed time of her meeting. A way too familiar face walked in, causing her to pause and suck in a deep breath.

Blake Peterson.

A rush of memories assailed her, his kiss vivid in her imagination. His timing couldn't have been more off, but there was nothing she could do about it, and dwelling on the kiss would do no good. The staff could fill his order and she would avoid a conversation with him altogether. It was better that way if she didn't want to set gossipy tongues wagging, or with Old Man Peterson watching her every move. Blake's grandfather was sure to be interested in his grandson's affairs.

She made her way to the backroom, pretending not to see him when he waved in her direction. At five minutes to two, she snuck a glance through the windowed swinging door that separated the shop floor from the back. Unfortunately, Blake had taken a seat in one of the booths. Doing a double-take, she rubbed her eyes to make sure she was seeing correctly. The image didn't change.

Mack Peterson and Blake were in the booth, the pair deep in conversation. She had no choice but to go out and join them if she didn't want to be late for her meeting with the senior Peterson.

They both looked up as she approached, ready smiles welcoming her.

"Good afternoon, gentleman. I'm sorry to interrupt, but I wanted to check in to let you know I'm available for our meeting whenever you're ready." She said this directly to Mr. Peterson, aiming for a confident air she wasn't feeling.

Blake shot a gaze between her and his grandfather, a scowl lining his face.

"I'm ready now," the older man said, nodding. "Have a seat, next to Blake, would you please?" His request was a bit odd, but who was she to object? Perhaps he wanted Blake to know about the promotion as well.

Yes. That had to be it.

She slid in next to Blake as he moved over, making sure to leave distance between them in the hopes his closeness didn't frazzle her brain cells. Not knowing what to expect, she needed to focus on something other than the handsome man next to her. "Thanks," she murmured.

"I've requested this meeting with each of you to discuss the future of Peterson's Ice Creamery. What you didn't know was that both of you would be here, so humor an old man and be agreeable. You both have vested interests in the shop, *and* I've come up with what I consider a fabulous plan. One that will help me decide the future of the creamery. As my first shop, it is dear to me."

Zoe frowned. This wasn't going at all like she expected.

"What's that supposed to mean, Grandpa? I thought you asked me to be here to discuss some renovation changes," Blake asked, clearly just as confused as she was.

The words *renovation changes* stuck in her brain and wouldn't let go. She hadn't known Mr. Peterson was even thinking of updating the place. And why would Blake, who hadn't lived in Hallbrook for years, be the one old man turned to for help?

"All your questions will be answered in time. Let's get a fresh cup of coffee and have a nice chat." He flagged one of the servers, and Lindsey came running right over to help.

"Hiya, Mr. Peterson. What can I get you?" she asked, her face wreathed in a genuine smile for the older man.

"Still keeping your grades up, young lady?" Mack's kindly smile and sincere question had the girl nodding.

"Yes, sir. Just like you told me to."

"Good. Good." He nodded. "We'll have three fresh cups of black coffee and then some privacy, if you will, please."

"Yes, sir. Coming right up." Lindsey was back with an extra cup for Zoe.

"Thanks," Zoe said, grateful she could hold the cup and hide her nerves.

Lindsey refilled the other's mugs to the top. "Let me know if you need anything else. Otherwise, I'll leave you to your meeting," she said before moving on to another table.

Grandpa cleared his throat. "Bright girl with a good future. I like to see that in the young folks today. Not enough of it if you ask me."

"She's a lovely person and a huge help here in the shop," Zoe added, putting in a good word for her. Mr. Peterson clearly had a soft spot for the girl, but then, with Lindsey, it was hard not to like her. Outgoing, smart, and funny. Not to mention, more confidence in her baby finger than Zoe had altogether.

"Wonderful. Let me start this meeting by saying, Zoe, that you've done an amazing job and your talents haven't gone unnoticed. This is why I'm considering you for the management position."

Considering meant he hadn't decided, which wasn't at all what she expected of this meeting. The proverbial chickens were coming back to peck at her. "Thank you, sir. I've been here a long time and always strive to do my best for the creamery and the customers." It couldn't hurt to put a plug in for herself, even if tooting her own horn didn't come naturally.

"I've noticed, trust me. As for you, Blake," he said, turning his gaze on his grandson, "I asked you home to help with some redesign ideas. I know you and your father don't see eye to eye, but I respect your talents and want to see what they could mean to the ice cream shop. I'm pleased you came home to make an old man happy, but I want your return to be more than a visit. I've never made any bones about it. Hallbrook is your home and where you belong."

"Thanks for caring enough to ask me to come home and present ideas; it's more than Dad has done. But I thought I was here to help with far more than the creamery. I'm anxious to prove to you how much better I can make things if you let me take the company into the new age. Dad will never agree, but with you on my side, there's a better chance of convincing him."

"You gotta start small, son. Let's start with the creamery and see where it goes. As to your dad, you leave him to me. He's stubborn, just like his old man was when he was his age." Mr. Peterson chuckled as he reflected on his own life. "But let's not get ahead of ourselves."

He took a sip of coffee and leaned back against the booth. "I want to have the ice cream shop renovated. As you know, the creamery is still under my direct control. I feel it's time to make some updated changes, and I'm looking for ideas. Blake, you're modern and high tech, whereas Zoe likes to keep with old traditions and values, something that's a huge hit with our clientele. I want to see what you both can come up with."

Blake looked at Zoe and then back at his grandfather, his scowl deepening. "Did you, or didn't you, ask me back here to draw up plans for the Peterson holdings?"

Zoe sucked in a deep breath, not like the direction of this conversation. Not one bit.

"And I thought we were here to discuss the manager's position you mentioned. Sorry, but I'm confused." Perhaps Blake's rebuttal gave her the confidence to speak up, or it was sheer insanity, but for once, her tongue functioned. Perhaps more than she'd have liked, but at least she'd laid her thoughts on the table.

"You're both right, in a way. Here's the deal," Mack said, his voice sharpening as he leaned forward, all sense of ease vanishing. Business Mack was in place. "I want to hold a renovation competition. I've thought this through, long and hard, and believe it's the answer to deciding the future of the creamery."

"What are you talking about?" Blake exclaimed.

"Team Blake and Team Zoe. I want you both to come up with a plan for how you would renovate the creamery, and the winner will lead the renovation changes and oversee the process the entire step of the way. Blake, it gives you the chance to show me what you've got with respect to Peterson Corporate holdings." He turned to her. "Zoe, this will give me the chance to see more of your management skills in action. And if you succeed, you will be given the manager title and a raise to go with it."

This was insanity. And totally not fair. The promotion should have been hers, without more hoops. Blake didn't know the first thing about the shop other than how to eat ice cream.

"Not exactly what I expected when I came home. Why should I have to compete for this?" Blake asked, scowling.

If she hadn't been blocking him in the booth, Zoe wasn't sure he wouldn't have bolted.

"Because Zoe is more talented than she gives herself credit for and I want her to reach for the stars, to become more confident. You, I want you to open yourself up to learn about the company holdings, and this gives me a chance to see how you would manage them. I built this company with heart and need to know who's on my side, and who's here simply to make a living."

Zoe couldn't argue the point about her own qualities—she did need more confidence. But it would have come in time with the job title. Surely Mr. Peterson knew she could handle the job without all this, for the lack of a better word, crazy contest.

"What's to stop me from going back to the city? I work for a company that is more than willing to pay me for what is considered state of the art designs. Modern technological advances are what keep a company ahead in the fight for customers," Blake insisted, his temper barely in check.

The problem was when it came to Blake, she felt bad for him, but at the same time, she agreed with his grandfather. Not that she liked the end result, but she understood his reasoning.

"That's making a living and my point. I want to see your heart and where it stands in the family business. I'm not getting any younger, and I've always had a soft spot for you. I'm giving you a chance to prove your place with Peterson's. I trust I won't be disappointed with your decision about whether to stay and take on this competition." Old Man Peterson was a tough old bird and not backing down under Blake's resistance.

Blake nodded. "Why not just give Zoe the promotion and let me redesign the place?"

"Good question—and the answer is that I want to see both your ideas. To know the possibilities and to have others weigh in with an opinion. I've decided the only way to be fair in my choice is to let the town council vote for which idea they like best, as well as your father and I. Nine votes in all, mine, of course, being the tie-breaker in the event one is needed."

Zoe tried to refocus. It's not like she had a choice. She would fight for the position she deserved. Besides, she already had some innovative ideas for fixing the place. She'd just never shared them with anyone. Now was her chance, and it came with the promise of the manager's job. "I'm in. What are the rules?"

"Thank you, Zoe. I was sure you'd rise to the challenge if pushed. And Blake, can I count on you?"

"Why not?" he asked, shaking his head to the contrary. "It's not as if you leave me much choice. I'll do it for you, but don't misunderstand my acquiescence. I don't like the idea of competing for my own family's business."

"Thank you, Blake. So, let's go over the rules," Mack said with a grin, ignoring Blake's last comment.

The old man had this all planned out, and Zoe was almost positive he never for a minute gave a thought that either of them wouldn't comply with the request. He glanced at his watch. "Actually, let's wait another five minutes for the rules, shall we? I don't want to have to go over them twice." Old Man Peterson chuckled. He was the only one laughing because, once again, he was speaking of things neither she nor Blake understood.

And then, of course, there was the red elephant in the room, or in her room anyway. Blake would hold a distinct advantage as heir to the Peterson Corporation, and there was no way it wouldn't play out in his favor.

The doorbell jingled. And then again. And again. Zoe frowned.

Odd time for a rush. She turned around in her seat to check out the newcomers to see if she'd need to pitch in and help serve. The rules of the competition would need to wait.

Except it wasn't customers walking in, but staff. Everyone on the payroll had shown up. All fifteen employees were now present, herself making all sixteen. She looked back at Mr. Peterson, who watched as the group moved to the register and spoke with Lindsey. She nodded in their direction, and everyone headed their way.

Mack Peterson stood. "Thanks for coming on such short notice, everyone. Double time for two hours on the clock to each of you for making an old man happy." He seemed more relaxed now than earlier, but then he should. He'd orchestrated a contest and had both her and Blake dancing to his tune.

The staff smiled and nodded, each one more than excited about the offer of extra pay.

"I've asked you all to come in to hear the rules of a competition I've set up, as each and every one of you will be involved."

Wait. What? The staff was part of the competition? Instead of clarifying things, they were getting more complicated. Zoe kept silent, waiting to hear the rest.

"What kind of competition, Mr. Peterson?" Brenda asked.

"Good question. It's a renovation competition. The team leaders are Blake Peterson, my grandson, and Zoe Carruthers, the assistant manager of the creamery and, I might add, your boss." He grinned. "They've agreed to design a plan for the renovation of the shop, and I want each of you to pick a side and join their team to assist them in the project."

"What's the catch?" one of the employees asked. It was either Keith or Teddy, but from where she sat, she couldn't tell.

"Another good question. Smart group." Mack nodded, holding up his hand to silence the increasing volume of discussions amongst them. "The catch is you need to pick wisely because the winning team will all be awarded one thousand dollars each and the team leader two thousand dollars as a bonus."

Mouths dropped open in silence and amazement, only to be quickly replaced by high fives and tremendous excitement.

"Is this for real?" Chad asked.

"Sure is, son." Old Man Peterson nodded. "The town council will make the decision, along with my son, Robert, and myself, making nine votes possible. Majority wins. The teams can begin meeting immediately, and the designs need to be turned over in two weeks' time. The Friday before Easter. The final announcement for a winner will be made at the annual company Easter dinner held at my place."

"So, the employees will pick which side they want to be on?" Zoe asked to clarify, dreading his answer. It was like dodgeball in school. She was never the popular girl and always the last to be picked, her sports abilities lacking. Everyone would pick Blake; why wouldn't they? Handsome, smart, and the Peterson heir; they'd be foolish to put their money eggs in her Easter basket.

"Yes. And now, I would like each of our team leaders to pitch a general concept of their vision to help you decide." The old man was enjoying this far too much.

The money would be an amazing blessing, one that would allow her to take Scott on a vacation to Disney World much sooner than she ever expected. For her, this competition was about a promotion, a raise, and now, the bonus. It was a chance to make a difference in her life. For Blake, it would be about winning. He didn't need the money. And Mr. Popular President of his class in high school would surely make lots of other people's dreams come true at the expense of hers.

Mack understood Zoe's need for more simple changes, but he'd pitted them against technology, and she wasn't sure where the town council would land. Her team, if anyone bothered to sign up, would have to work extra hard to figure out the details.

Blake's demeanor was already changing right before her very eyes. His happy smile back in place, they both slid out of the booth to make their presentation. Something else Blake excelled at—the limelight.

For Zoe, change wasn't good. For her, simple was always better, something she'd have to explain to others. But what she wouldn't explain was why. That was her forever secret. Zoe had convinced her mother to let her redecorate her bedroom, and they'd had fun together. That was until her father walked in and saw it—the night he left. *Money ill-spent on a perfectly good room.* That's how her father had seen it anyway.

There'd been nothing about making a young girl's dreams come true as her mother had done. Something her father managed to ruin for Zoe in less than twenty-four hours. It was a memory she'd hated and struggled to repress to no avail.

What did change, however, was Zoe's own perception of what happened that night. As an adult, she'd come to the realization her parents had far more marital problems than she'd believed for years. That fateful night her father left had only been the final straw in the failed marriage.

Just like her marriage with Larry had been fraught with problems before it came to a crashing halt.

Chapter Four

♥

B LAKE STILL COULDN'T BELIEVE his grandfather had tricked him. The promise of a meeting to go over his innovative ideas had been enough to get him to Hallbrook, but it would seem nothing had changed.

A competition. The very idea rankled his nerves, knowing what it really meant—they were still waiting for him to prove his worth in the family business.

And to make matters worse, his grandfather had pitted him against the beautiful and alluring Zoe Carruthers. The woman he'd kissed only a few nights ago. And a woman whose kisses kept him hoping for more. Not that she was his type.

It was just a one-off moment, and a repeat would prove it to him. The problem, however, was Zoe herself had laid out some clear boundaries. And now, his grandfather had set them up against each other. Which meant spending more time with her, but with each hoping to win for their own reasons. There was no room for attraction.

He pasted on a broad smile, something he'd learned to do a long time ago when the need arose. Outspoken friendliness was the key to winning, just not something he enjoyed doing. *It was an act.* One he'd learned to perfect in high school, and one he'd call upon again at this moment.

"Ladies first, Zoe. I pride myself on being a gentleman," he said, shooting her a wink, hoping to disarm her. Anything to help his cause because Zoe was filling his head with ideas that had nothing to do with the competition and everything to do with her. It had to be the novelty of close contact with the fresh face, ponytail look. Blake was used to dealing with progressive ideas, and that included progressive women. Chic women, not country bumpkins.

"Thank you, Blake. Don't mind if I do."

So much for rattling her with limited time to think things through.

Zoe glanced at his grandfather, and when he nodded, she turned back to face the employees. "You all work with me and know me quite well. We know the customers, and we understand them. For me, an ice cream shop is a wonderful place for families to come, visitors from out of town to stop in, or anyone looking for a treat to satisfy their sweet tooth. A lot people view going to their favorite ice cream parlor as a tradition.

"I see soda fountains, red leather seats at the bar, shiny silver metal gleaming back at you, and booths that encourage friendly chatter and memory-making fun. I see a nostalgic look that shows a fresh and updated look into the past. And Team Zoe will welcome any ideas and members who embrace the *olden days'* of the creamery in this town and wish to preserve its sweet uniqueness. Together, we can make this place sparkle and shine with newness but keep it rich with history."

The employees clapped and nodded.

Not a good sign for Blake. Zoe was comfortable speaking with the employees, something he hadn't counted on. When she was in her comfort zone, her confidence levels rose to heights he hadn't witnessed on the eve of her birthday. *This was a different Zoe.* Better, but still, her country freshness exuded from every pore.

Blake held up his hand. "Thank you, Zoe. Well done." He beamed at her, his gaze taking in her flushed features. Maybe her confidence wasn't as high as he first assumed.

"If you join Team Blake, on the other hand, you will be choosing a team that embraces modernization. Glitz. Glamor. Fun. Energy. These are my buzz words. Ice cream is sugar and all about the rush, so I say let's give the customers what they're coming for. Not just ice cream, but modern-day fun. Change is excitement just around the corner, and that's what I hope Team Blake and its members will bring to Peterson's Ice Creamery."

The employees clapped and nodded.

His grandfather stepped forward. "You've heard from both team leaders. Take a few minutes to decide. Each employee needs to speak up clearly to announce which team you chose."

The employees moved off, bits and pieces of their conversation drifting his way.

Blake had kept his speech short and simple but felt like he was back in high school running for class president. He'd only run to get the attention of the popular girl in his class, and after he'd won and she'd gone out with him, things didn't turn out like he planned. Tammy wasn't such a nice girl, and it hadn't taken long for him to realize the gentlemanly thing to do was let her break it off. To make that happen, he'd thrown himself into class politics and being progressive in his ideas to avoid spending time with her. Eventually, she'd dumped him, but the progressive way of thinking stuck.

The lesson he'd learned after years of being teased in school about the way he smelled because of growing up on a farm, was that a false air of confidence couldn't be discerned from the truth. No one understood that it was all a cover for him, and Blake planned on keeping it that way.

For years, he'd tried to convince his own family that progress on the farm would be good. He knew from firsthand experience how easily machines could replace human chores forced upon children, saving them from a humiliating and painful school life, and it was something he wanted to bring to Peterson's.

Except his father continued to fight him every step of the way. Unfortunately, his grandfather's request to see his designs and hear his ideas didn't come as straightforward as Blake had planned. But he'd do this—and he'd win. And it would prove to his father and grandfather that he was ready to join the family business.

"Times up," his grandfather called out a short five minutes later. "Form a line, and one by one, pick a team. Remember, choose wisely as one thousand dollars, and the pride of being on the winning team are at stake."

Blake grinned and waved politician style. The outward appearance of *I've got this* was a must. In a way, he felt sorry for Zoe, knowing the odds were somewhat stacked in his favor. But this was his family business, not hers, and being a respected member of the family was important to him.

"Team Blake." The first employee announced, stepping toward Blake's side of the room.

"Team Blake." The next employee shot an *I'm sorry* look at Zoe before joining Blake's team.

"Team Blake." One more employee joined his team.

Blake shot a glance at Zoe, noting that she was biting her lower lip. The strain of people choosing sides was taking its toll on her. A guilty feeling washed over him. He remembered what it was like to be last chosen for teams. Maybe he shouldn't have turned on the friendly appeal as strong as he had. Please, he prayed, let the next one be for Zoe.

"Team Zoe," the girl said, smiling at Zoe as she crossed to her side. The two women joined hands as though they were a force to reckon with.

The rest of the employees chose a team, and when it was over, the total amounted to Team Blake—thirteen members, and Team Zoe—four members. Two to one, the employees had voted for him. The question was, were they voting for his progressive ideas or for the family name? He wasn't a superstitious man by any means, but the fact his team had thirteen members crossed his mind as unlucky. Utter nonsense, he chided himself.

"Okay, now that the teams are established, Blake and Zoe, you can start to organize and plan with your teammates. And Lindsey, you'll have to catch up a little later as some customers are coming in. Thank you all for indulging me on this meeting. I want this to be fun. *A friendly competition.* Let's see how well everyone works together and come up with some great ideas."

"Thank you for this opportunity, sir. Our team won't let you down," Zoe said. It would seem the schmoozing had already begun. Blake would be a fool to underestimate his opponent. There would only be one winner, and he intended to be it.

"Thanks, Grandpa. This was a great idea and judging by the size of my team, progressive and futuristic are a solid vote. We look forward to sharing our new vision with the town council and you." He intentionally left out his father because he knew that vote was already lost to Zoe. Anything that wasn't a vote for his own son would be his father's choice.

"I look forward to seeing both designs. Zoe, I'm sure Blake will be around a lot the next two weeks, so please, make sure to give him free access to the shop to keep the playing field level." His grandfather's suggestion made sense, and Blake was relieved it wouldn't be a problem.

"Absolutely. Visit anytime, Blake. In fact, I think you should learn the ropes here. Talk and serve customers. Make ice cream. You know, just so you have a solid foundation for what you're designing," Zoe offered, a wide grin on her face. "We can always use the extra help."

"I don't think—"

"That's a great idea, Zoe," his grandfather said, cutting him off. "Expect him here in the morning, bright and early." The old man's smile meant he was up to something, and Blake needed to figure it out.

"Make that Monday morning, and you've got a deal. I'll do whatever it takes since it's for the betterment of the family business." He didn't have time for this nonsense, but he'd learned how to play the game a long time ago.

"Okay, then. Now that we have that settled, I guess I'll leave you both to your leadership duties." His grandfather waved and headed out the front door, his exit followed closely by an eruption of talk and laughter.

The employees were all in on this competition, more than likely already counting on having the golden ticket to a thousand dollars.

Or in Zoe's case, two thousand. He couldn't help but wonder what she would use it for and planned to ask her when he got a chance. It would help him to understand her better and to know what was at stake besides the promotion.

As for Blake, he had far more invested in the competition than money.

Long after Mack Peterson left, Zoe and her team discussed options. It was a small group, but she was grateful anyone had signed on with her. Her initial fear after hearing the first three choose Blake was that no one would pick her. That would have been humiliation at its finest.

But Lindsey, Teddy, and Tony had picked her team, and their ideas were outstanding. Each one had a research assignment by the time they left, Lindsey mostly listening and chiming in with her thoughts in between customers.

Together they hammered out a plan, one that would enhance options to take nostalgia to new heights while retaining the historical feel of the creamery. It left her excited about the possibilities of a win, even against the family advantage Blake had. Of course, she also realized the town council would be fair in their votes. She just didn't know where Robert Peterson would land, or Old Man Peterson for that matter.

Zoe hadn't known about the rift between Blake and his father, but it helped her to understand why he stayed away from Hallbrook. She wouldn't have liked living under the disapproval of someone all the time. And the fact it was Blake, a guy who was used to popularity, and of course, success in everything he did, was a double whammy. Whether Blake knew it or not, his grandfather followed his achievements closely and was quick to tell whoever would listen about his grandson's accolades.

But it didn't change a thing for her—this time, Blake had to lose. It was best for the ice cream shop, and best for her and Scott. A vacation had always seemed a long way off, but now, it was within reach.

Her son would be thrilled to finally have his dream visit to Disney World come true.

Not that she'd tell him about the competition and get his hopes up. Zoe couldn't bear his disappointment if she didn't win, especially not on top of everything else she'd lose if her designs weren't selected as the winners.

Chapter Five

♥

BLAKE WORKED THE REST of Friday and most of Saturday on some of his projects from the office. Just because he was home didn't mean his regular workload had lessened. Far too often, the creative focus simply wasn't there, his brain more on the creamery and the competition, and therefore, Zoe.

Her sweet smile and zest toward everything she did had been reflected in the animated way she addressed her team. Not that he should have noticed, but when some of his group were tossing out ideas, his gaze seemed to drift in her direction. It had to be because of the kiss. A second kiss would prove she wasn't his type, and there was nothing special about her. The women he dated were all too quick to offer kisses, and he easily grew bored. Zoe's denial of a second kiss was all that left him hanging. It was the only thing that made sense.

Thinking about her was a condition he needed to rectify, and the easiest way to do that was to go on a date. With someone other than Zoe. He poured over the names in his address book, settled on Tracy Summerton. Lancaster's mayor's daughter, a woman who had glitz and glamour perfected, and would be perfect for an evening's distraction.

Tracy had been thrilled to hear from him and, of course, accepted his invitation. Except, after hanging up, his focus wasn't improving. Blake gave up and headed out to the barn, hoping to get more ideas for some of the processes he could improve with technology.

"Come on, Hank. Let's go for a walk to your favorite place." Blake chuckled when the black and white dog bounded off the couch and headed in his direction. After a quick body shake, the dog settled at Blake's feet, eager to go.

The two of them had been a pair now for over two years, and Hank had become his confidant. The dog was easy to talk to and rarely answered, and when he did, it was only to agree with a bark. His furry friend had heard it all. Life and its shortcomings were frequent subjects of discussion, at least from Blake's perspective anyway. Otherwise, Hank's daily routine was a series of naps, curled up on the couch or, much to Blake's chagrin, his bed. The apartment where he lived in the city wasn't exactly heaven for the mutt he'd rescued from the side of the road.

Blake had never understood how people could dump animals off like that. His first response had been to take the dog to a shelter, but somewhere between the roadside stop and the shelter, his heart and brain flip-flopped. It had been an adjustment period, but Blake loved Hank and his undivided devotion. Of course, it meant extra preparation time for work in order to take Hank for his morning walk, but it also gave Blake the much-needed inspiration for a morning run. They were the perfect pair.

Heading for the kitchen and the back-door exit, Blake realized he'd picked the wrong path when he spotted his father eating lunch.

"Going somewhere?" his father asked, barely lowering the paper he was reading.

"Out to the barn. Hank needs a run." Blake reached for the door, hoping for a quick escape. He wasn't in the mood for another lecture.

"The stalls need mucking, and the ice rink needs to be scraped, and the cows need to be fed. I'm behind schedule. Think you could manage any of those things to help your old man out?" The hardened expression on his dad's face spoke volumes. It was the same old story between them, which is why Blake didn't come home. His father was never happy to see him, only to figure out how much work he could do around the place. Forget the fact Blake already had a job. And now with the competition and so much at stake, it wasn't something he would volunteer to do, even if he wanted to.

"That's what you have employees for. The cows can be fed by a timed feeder if you'd let me design and install one. And there are machines for the rink if you'd buy one. Seems to me you'd enjoy the benefits of progress if you tried." If his father could ask for help, Blake could put in his two cents.

"My answer is still no. A man's worth is determined by his daily output in work. Hard work. Work that builds character—not progress." His cutting remark hit home the same as it always did. Blake was a soft city boy in his dad's old-fashioned opinion.

"And so is mine. I've got a date tonight and have no intention of going on one with the stench of manure. Thanks, but no thanks."

"That's why we have showers but suit yourself. Your sister will be home soon; maybe she'll help me." His dad picked up his sandwich and took a bite, turning away and ending the discussion. Sarah liked farm work almost as little as he did. But then, as the only girl in the family, she hadn't been the one required to work in the barn every morning and every afternoon.

Blake left through the kitchen door, frustrated with the hard and fast methods his dad insisted on using and his close-minded attitude toward new ideas. It was why he'd been surprised when his grandfather called him home. His dad ran the day-to-day operations of the Peterson Corporation, but his grandfather had the final say so—in everything.

He'd given up daily control but kept fifty-one percent of the company, giving his father the other forty-nine percent. It was something else his father hadn't liked but had been forced to accept. Not to mention, the creamery was listed separately as a Peterson holding, his grandfather keeping one-hundred percent interest as his first business, and the place he'd met Blake's grandmother.

Woof. Woof. Hank ran ahead toward the barn, eager to play with whatever animal he could. There were a few cats he liked to chase, and then there was the new calf that was three times Hank's size. He didn't seem to mind though, maybe because the calf looked like Hank, white with black splotches scattered all over.

Blake moved off, carefully watching where he walked. He waved at several of the employees, although not having been home in years, he couldn't associate names and faces. Taking out a pocket pad he used for ideas, Blake sketched out the barn layout, something he'd use to draw the design on the computer later. His father wouldn't be happy if he knew Grandpa had asked to see some of his ideas. Correction, his grandfather wanted creamery designs, not ideas for modernizing the barn. But Blake wouldn't let this opportunity go by to present him with both.

His grandfather would stand up to his dad, no doubt, if push came to shove, but Blake wasn't so sure his dad would accept any change without a fight. And Blake wasn't here to cause a rift between the two, only to help and establish his own place within the family business. So far, no one needed him, or at least not the talents he offered. Designing technology to improve output and lower expenses tapped into his creative side, the spreadsheet effects on income appealing to his left-brain's need to play with numbers.

Blake walked out the layout of the barn, drawing it in small sections and making notes as needed. Hank followed him, alternately playing, digging in the straw, and agitating the cows. By the time Blake was finished, the dog was nowhere to be found. Not that Blake was worried. Hank would show up when he was good and ready, the smells and sights a drawcard far stronger than Blake's city apartment had ever been.

Glancing at his watch, he hadn't realized so much time had passed. Hurrying back to the main house, he headed for his room to change clothes. Tracy would take one look at him in his jeans and boots and run for daddy and the golf club to find a more suitable companion for the evening. After a quick shower, he changed into a suit, tucking in his shirt and adjusting his tie. Dabbing on a small bit of cologne just in case there were any lingering effects of his barn visit, he checked his appearance in the mirror.

Satisfied, he moved to the closet and found his Italian leather loafers to complete the professional, confident, and modern look he desired. Clothes, after all, make the man. Inside, he wasn't that guy, but outside, he had that down to a tee.

He headed outside to call the dog in. "Hank," he hollered. "Here, boy." Blake gave a loud whistle.

There was still no sign of the dog. Blake stepped off the porch and went around the house to call him again. It was unusual for his faithful friend not to come running when he heard his name. "Hank!" he hollered again. Blake walked a few steps toward the barn, just as Hank bounded around the corner of the building, headed straight for him. "Whoa, boy,"

Blake said as the dog came charging, his excitement and energy in overload.

Blake turned away slightly, hoping to keep him from jumping on his suit. His foot slipped, and he tried to regain his balance just as Hank came to a stop next to him. Thankfully the dog didn't jump on him with his dirty paws. He reached down to pet Hank. "Good boy. It's time to go inside. I've got a hot date tonight." Blake grinned, scratching behind the dog's ears.

A whiff of manure reached his nose. "Please tell me you didn't roll in the poop. I don't have time to clean you up or to change." He shook his head as he looked the dog over, checking his paws one by one. "Nothing. Good boy."

Blake headed for the house to let the dog in, the strong odor of manure sticking with him. He opened the door and Hank barreled inside to the warmth and comfort. Blake turned to leave, the sight of a deep brown stain on one step stopping him cold. Glancing down at his shoes, he grimaced. It wasn't Hank who'd stepped in the nasty stuff; it was him.

Gross. His fine leather shoes weren't so fine anymore. Making his way around to the spigot on the side of the house, he scuffed his feet on the ground along the way, trying to rub the excess sludge off. Grabbing a stick, he turned up his foot and started to dig at whatever was still lodged in the cracks of the sole. Most of it came off to his relief. He grabbed the hose and turned on the water, determined to get every last trace of the manure and the smell gone.

Blake took the sprayer and pointed it at his shoe. Pulling back the lever, the water sprayed with an unexpected force, hitting his shoe and blasting it everywhere. Including on him—and his suit. "Just great," he said, shaking his head. He was already late leaving, but he'd have to be a little later.

There was no way the suit would dry, and it looked as though he'd peed his pants. Not a pretty sight. Back in his room, Blake chose another suit, changed, and then added another splash of cologne for good measure. One could never be too safe when it came to fresh farm odors.

Satisfied with his appearance, Blake glanced at his watch. He'd be fifteen minutes late, but knowing Tracy, she'd be twenty minutes late anyway. Fashionably late they called it. And for once, he'd be the one taking advantage of the rule.

In the living room, Sarah looked up and whistled. "Don't you look dashing. No wonder the ladies like having you around." She laughed. "Mr. GQ, if you ask me."

"I didn't ask." He'd never been comfortable with compliments. Especially ones from Sarah, since she was his sister. "Don't have time to talk. See you later."

"Where you off to?" she asked as he neared the door.

"I have a date for your information." He shot her a grin, knowing how she felt about his dating principles.

"Oh, right. Dad did mention something about that. Poor girl doesn't know you don't do serious." Sarah scrunched up her face in distaste.

"Sure, she does. We've gone out before."

"You're breaking your never-date-the-same-woman-twice rule? Wow, she must be special."

"Hardly. It was a while back, but I'm sure she remembers I don't do relationships." Blake reached for the door. He was late enough as it was without standing around to chit chat with his sister.

"Whatever you say. One day, you'll fall for someone. I just hope they don't play by your rules and break your heart. By the way, you sure got Dad riled up this afternoon. What happened?"

"You know Dad, it's always the same old story with him. But if Grandpa likes my ideas, he'll be singing a different tune." He glanced around to make sure he hadn't been overheard.

"Be careful, Blake. It's a fine line you're walking, but one I hope you make it to the other side. Preferably without falling off."

"Thanks, sis. Got to run." Blake hurried out the door and to his Porsche. Sliding in, he turned the key to fire up the engine, loving the smooth purr as it came to life every time he started the car. Except nothing happened. He tried again, this time stepping on the gas. Nothing.

Now what? Blake slammed his hand against the steering wheel. It was as though fate were trying to keep him from going on a date with Tracy. Except that would be ridiculous. He didn't believe in fate, but he did believe in a malfunctioning machine. And the manure—well, that was his own fault.

Nothing on the car dashboard was lit up, and there was no clicking sound. And his biggest problem was that for all the knowledge he had about technical designing, he was clueless when it came to automobiles and their engines. Getting out of the car, he slammed the door and headed back inside the house.

Sarah looked up. "What's wrong? Forget something? Like your keys." She grinned, having far too much fun at his expense.

"My car won't start. Not that you care," Blake said, scowling at his little sister with her singsong not-a-care-in-the-world attitude.

"Fancy, expensive machine like that ought to work when you want it to if you ask me."

"I agree," he snapped. It might not be her fault, but enough was enough.

"You could take Grandpa's old truck. I know he ran into town and is using the car. I'm sure he won't mind. It might need some cleaning first, but surely your date will wait. It's you, after all."

Blake shook his head, the image of Tracy's face lined with abject horror if he dared pulled up in front of her house in the old rusty truck too much to bear. He'd be the laughingstock of her and her friends. Image was everything, and he'd worked hard on perfecting his. "Very funny, but I'll pass. Not sure my date could handle the old Ford." He grimaced.

"Suit yourself." Sarah shrugged, looking inordinately pleased before she turned her focus back to her magazine.

There was nothing else he could do. Thirty minutes late and arriving in a beat-up Ford would never work. He dialed Tracy's number as he headed down the hall, determined to change out of his suit.

"Hello, Blake. I was expecting you to pick me up, not call. Why aren't you here yet? I've been ready for ages," Tracy drawled.

Blake steeled himself for the conversation and Tracy's displeasure at the change in plans. "I'm sorry to have to do this, but I need to break our date."

"What? How dare you?" she ground out.

He pushed the phone away from his ear, her angry voice much louder than her fake sweet side. "I'm having car trouble. It's not like I have any control over the situation."

"Now what am I supposed to do for the night? I simply can't sit at home like a loser. Of all the—"

"That's enough, Tracy. It's not like I planned this. I'm sure you'll find something or someone to entertain you. Have a good night." A few choice unladylike words burnt the phone lines as Blake hung up. Being stood up wasn't something she dealt with often.

So much for an entertaining evening.

Blake changed into a clean pair of jeans and a sweater and grabbed his overcoat from the closet. He headed back into the living room. "Any chance you want to go into town with me and catch dinner at Sally's?" he asked Sarah, figuring the two of them could do some catching up. "I've just need to make one quick stop first."

"Thanks, but no. I've got a date with Dalton."

At least one of them would have an enjoyable evening out, and not a lonely one. He'd have to call the local mechanic to figure out what ailed his car.

Grabbing the keys off the board in the kitchen, Blake headed for the old truck.

Of course, *it* started on the first try.

Chapter Six

♥

SARAH'S SPUR OF THE moment offer to meet at Sally's Diner was exactly what Zoe needed after a long day at work. The biting cold had Zoe and Scott making a beeline for the place after she parked. Once inside, she looked around for her friend. There was no sign of her yet, and they grabbed the only available booth at the back of the diner. Saturday was a busy time for Hallbrook residents to go out on the town, which inevitably included a stop at Sally's or O'Malley's.

Christina, Sally's granddaughter, arrived to take their order almost instantly, handing them a menu, and flipping her pad open. "Chicken pot pie is tonight's special. If you're ready to order, I'm ready." With purple hair and a nose ring, and sporting a couple of tattoos, the girl was on remote control with a bored attitude to boot.

"We're waiting on one more person, but we'd both like an iced tea. Sweet, please."

"Two sweet teas. Gotcha." Christina flipped her pad closed and shoved it into the pocket of her apron, sliding the pen to the top of her ear before walking off.

"What are you thinking of having tonight, honey?" she asked her son. He'd been out-of-sorts lately, and she was hoping a night out would help him bounce back.

"I don't know. I reckon the pot pie is fine." Scott leaned forward, putting his elbows on the table to hold his head up.

"I'm thinking the same thing. Two great minds thinking alike." She ruffled his thick brown hair, earning her a pull back.

"Mom, that's for kids. I'm not a kid anymore."

"You're nine. Plenty of time to be a kid."

"Whatever. Can I play a game on your phone while we wait for Sarah and my dinner?" If he didn't get his way, he'd just cold-shoulder her anyway. Larry used to play video games all the time, and

Scott had the same penchant for playing as his father. Not that he'd admit it. Ever since Scott's father walked out when he was six, her son had been dismissive of Larry. Not to mention protective of Zoe. It wasn't often he shut her out like this, and in time, she knew whatever was bothering him would come out. It always did.

She'd learned early on to be patient with her son. Zoe handed him her phone. "Only until the meal arrives."

He shrugged and took the phone from her, accessing the special tab she'd created for him with several carefully selected G-rated games.

Zoe glanced around the place, waving at a few people she knew. The bell jingled over the door as another customer sauntered in. Instantly recognizing Blake, she waved at him as he glanced in her direction. Too late, she realized he'd misread her wave, and now he was headed in her direction. All six-foot solid hunk of him. He'd been in a suit at the party and at the creamery, but now he was dressed in jeans and a sweater, and he fit right in and looked darn good doing it. More relaxed, truth be told.

"Good evening, Zoe. Place is packed. Tell me my timing is perfect and that you're leaving?" he asked, grinning down at her.

"Wow. Hello to you too. I think. What did I do to you that you want me gone so badly?" she teased, unable to help herself. She knew what he meant but wasn't letting him off the hook so easily.

"Sorry, I didn't mean it that way. I meant—"

"I know how you meant it. The place is full, and you were hoping this booth would be available if Scott and I were on our way out." She flashed him a smile. "But, unfortunately, tonight's not your lucky night. We just got here."

"You can say that again," Blake said, rolling his eyes.

"Actually, we're waiting on Sarah."

"Uh, Mom. A text message just popped up on your phone from Sarah. It says she's got to cancel."

"She's the one that set this up in the first place." Zoe frowned.

"Well, then, I'll just mosey on down to O'Malley's. This place is packed and there's no telling when someone will leave. You two have a nice evening." Blake dipped his head in a farewell nod.

"Wait," she said, reaching for his arm.

Blake paused and took a step back. "What is it?"

"Why don't you join us for dinner?" she offered. It was insanity, but the offer was out before she could stop it.

"Are you sure? I wouldn't want to intrude on your family night out."

"You don't mind, do you, Scott?"

Her son looked up from his game, a scowl on his face. "Actually, I do."

"Scott!" she scolded.

"You asked, I answered." His nose scrunched in distaste as he looked Blake up and down, his shoulders going back and tensing. If Zoe didn't know any better, she'd say her son had puffed up, as if sizing up Blake and finding him wanting. But Scott didn't even know Blake as far as she knew. *But he had witnessed the kiss.*

"Well, it's not the right answer. The place is packed, and Blake is a—"

"Friend. Actually, we're competitors in a contest, and this would be a great time to discuss how we're going to get through next week."

"Competitors in what?" Scott asked, suddenly interested.

"You didn't tell him?" Blake asked her.

"No. There was no reason to. I wouldn't want to get his hopes up for nothing," Zoe said, glaring at Blake, willing him to shut up on the subject.

"Tell me what? And why would I get my hopes up? We don't keep secrets, Mom. About anything." He hurled the last part at her as if she'd committed some grave offense. It was only the contest.

She resigned herself to explaining as there was no way to extricate herself without relaying some of the information. "There's a contest at work for redesigning the creamery, and Blake and I are team leaders."

"As in working together?" He scowled.

"Quite the opposite. We're on opposing teams," Blake said, a slight grin on his face.

"Then you don't need to work together. Guess there's no reason for you to eat with us," Scott said defiantly.

"Scott Carruthers, you need to knock off the rudeness. Blake, please excuse his poor manners, and if you dare, please, join us for dinner." It hadn't been the best of ideas, but Scott's attitude pushed her to get Blake to accept. Her son needed to understand she wouldn't condone his attitude, and it certainly wouldn't help him get his way.

"If you're sure it's okay, then I'm game. Might be nice to have company for dinner."

"Scott, come sit next to me and let Mr. Peterson have that side."

Her son snatched up the phone, slid out of the booth, and plopped himself down next to her, his scowl firmly in place. Slouching back against the seat, he proceeded to play the game he'd started, completely ignoring her. This was going to be one of those long nights. Even longer once they got home and discussed his behavior.

Christina came back with the two teas. "I see your friend arrived. Are you ready to order?" It wasn't worth correcting the server that it wasn't the friend she'd expected at all. Hopefully, people wouldn't get the wrong idea. Small town—big gossips.

"Almost. Here, Blake," she said, handing him the menu. "We'll order while you decide."

He took the menu and nodded.

"Scott and I will have the chicken pot pie special, with a side salad. Ranch dressing for him and the balsamic vinaigrette for me," Zoe rattled off the order.

"Got it. And for you," she asked Blake, turning toward him.

"I'll have what Zoe's having. Sounds good. And water to drink," he added, handing Christina the menu.

"Coming right up." The girl turned and left, stopping at the next table to clear some plates.

It would seem Blake wouldn't have had to wait long, but this was okay. Or, at least, she hoped it was. It would be better if they figured out a way to get along during this competition as they'd be around each other a lot. It's not as if they had to be bitter rivals or anything.

Scott was still busy playing his game and ignoring them both.

"Why is a handsome, single guy like yourself eating alone on a Saturday night?" Zoe asked. The question had been on the tip of her tongue since he'd arrived.

"I'm not alone. I'm with you," he said, his voice lowering a notch to a husky drawl.

Scott looked up at him and then at her, shaking his head. "Grown-ups. Get real, will you? That's my mom."

"There's nothing wrong with teasing your mother, young man. It's just in fun, and she knows it." Blake didn't seem in the least offended. He seemed to take it in stride.

"Whatever," Scott huffed and returned to his game.

Scott had been acting up ever since her party, and it could only mean one thing—the kiss she shared with Blake had him rattled. And she hadn't found the right time to discuss it with him yet, or at the very least clarify it was only a birthday kiss. Zoe knew better, but her son didn't need to know all the details. She'd have to talk to him later and put him at ease. She and Blake were not together, nor would they be. Ever. Talk about two people from opposite sides of the track. The Petersons were wealthy and influential, and she...well, she wasn't. A clear case of the haves and the have-nots.

"So to answer your question, more seriously," Blake said, cocking his head to one side with a grin in an effort to draw Scott into the fun of things, "I'm alone tonight because of a failed date."

"What happened?" She couldn't help but laugh at his antics, and her curiosity was brimming over.

"The story starts with manure, moves on to a soaked suit, and then to a car that wouldn't start. My date didn't appreciate the over-the-top fashionably late approach, but I reckon it's the pickup truck that did her in when I mentioned our ride." Blake was laughing as he recounted the evening, not at all embarrassed to share the ill-fated evening with her.

"I'm so sorry I asked. How awful. But what's wrong with a truck?"

Scott had stopped playing his game and was watching Blake, listening to the conversation.

"Let's just say she was expecting the Porsche, and a classic, somewhat rusty Ford was a poor substitute." Blake chuckled, something he did often around her.

"I guess that depends on your date. I would have loved the experience," Zoe said. She enjoyed all things old because they came with stories and memories.

"Of course, you would, Miss Nostalgia and let's revive history."

"You have a Porsche?" Scott asked, unable to remain standoffish.

"I do. A black and sleek finely tuned machine. Most of the time, anyway." Blake shook his head and grinned.

"Cool. I mean, I guess that's cool if you're into that sort of thing. But my mom and I aren't, are we, Mom?" Her son looked at her for confirmation.

"I'd have to agree with you, Scott. But then I've never had the chance to ride in a Porsche, or any new sports car for that matter, so what would I know." Her pleasure in Scott's sudden interest was short-lived as he returned his focus to the game, but now, Zoe knew her son was listening. *His secret was out.*

"Maybe I'll take you for a spin some afternoon. Give us a break from all work and no play routine."

"Thanks, I think." Zoe grinned, excited at the prospect but not wanting to show it. "It's a shame about your date." She wanted to know more, her interest far greater than it should be.

"She'll get over it. If not, there are plenty of others all too willing to go out with me. Women who understand the rules." Of course, there were. Why wouldn't there be? Mr. GQ would have a line of highfalutin women fawning over him.

"Rules?" she squeaked out, almost hating to ask. This conversation had suddenly taken an interesting turn.

"I'm not looking for a wife. I find relationships become boring after a short bit, so why go down that road? I make sure the women I date understand it's just dinner and dancing." He shrugged.

Blake was most definitely the wrong kind of man for her, just like she'd already surmised. "Jaded attitude, but it's your life." Zoe shrugged.

"What about you?" he asked, leaning back against the cushioned back of the booth.

She shook her head and nodded toward Scott. Not a conversation she was willing to have in front of her son. Besides, how did you tell someone your first husband got bored with family life and small-town living in Hallbrook and deserted you for a fast pace life in the city with single women. *A life that sounded eerily like Blake's.* Zoe wanted true love and happiness, but not at the expense of her son or her own beliefs. "I prefer to talk about the ice cream shop."

"Fair enough," he said, shaking his head in understanding. "So why the nostalgic approach, if you don't mind my asking?"

This was a subject she had plenty to say about. "People in this town don't typically move away. There are lots of generational families, and the place is rich with history. The ice cream shop is one of the first stores that opened, and everyone here has a special memory or two. I would hate to see that destroyed, so instead, I'll find a way to embrace the old in a fresh way."

"But even if we lose some customers with progressive renovations, new customers will arrive on the scene and appreciate the faster service. Which means we can service more customers, and the bottom line grows." Blake was serious, and it wasn't a compliment. Not when it came to the creamery. He had it all wrong.

"It's not a dine and dash, Blake." She frowned, not liking the image he painted at all. When it came to redesigning the creamery, they were on opposite ends of the spectrum, and there was no clear way to make both ideas work. Someone had to lose.

"This also isn't the 1800s," he quipped.

Christina approached carrying a large tray perfectly balanced, and a clear signal it was time to change the conversation.

"Let's agree to disagree and enjoy our meal," Zoe said, watching the girl hand out their plates of food. "Scott, it's time to eat, and you need to give me the phone."

Her son looked about to refuse but thought better of it. Luckily. This wasn't the place for a showdown, especially not in front of Blake.

Chapter Seven

♥

OTHER THAN A FEW walks in the woods with Hank, Blake had spent Sunday working on transferring his hand-sketched drawing of the barn to the computer. Not to mention avoiding Sarah and her non-stop questions about his evening with Zoe. Sarah had warned him away from her friend, but unfortunately, Zoe lost no time telling his sister they dined together. It's not as if it were his fault Sarah had canceled out in the first place. Otherwise, they could have all eaten together, and she'd have been there to supervise.

And therein lay the crux of the matter.

Sarah had told him she had a date with Dalton. Then she'd set up a date with Zoe—after Blake mentioned he was headed to Sally's. It was something worth considering, although only days ago,

Sarah had warned him away from Zoe. Either it was a simple matter of crossed wires or Sarah was up to something. Odds were against Sarah, knowing his sister's penchant for meddling.

Monday morning was a welcome change of pace, and he was dressed and ready to meet up with the lovely Zoe and see what she had in store for him. How hard could it be to make ice cream and serve it in a dish? She'd made sure to remind him he would be working in the shop and to wear casual clothes. AKA jeans and a clean shirt, but no suit. Going to work without a suit on left him off balance. His power suits and ties were part of the outward confidence he liked to portray.

Blake grabbed the truck keys and headed for the door.

Woof. Woof.

"Sorry, Hank, not this time, buddy. I'll be home for lunch to let you back out." He rubbed the dog's ears and patted his back, trying to appease the hurt look that appeared. In the city apartment, the dog slept a lot and didn't seem to mind waiting for their scheduled walks, but ever since they'd arrived here, it was like the country smells were calling his name.

Truth be told, Blake was enjoying the slower pace, even though it meant dealing with his dad. Which wasn't often since his father worked all day and was rarely at the house.

He'd moved back in the old farmhouse after Blake's mother died, sharing the place with his grandfather. Which usually meant early to bed and always early to rise. Glancing over at the skating rink area in front of the barn revealed not a soul in sight. An anomaly any other time of the day in the winter. It wouldn't be long, and the temperatures would grow warm enough to shut down the place, and the town's major source of entertainment would be gone until next winter.

His car was in the driveway, pulled off to the side and out of the way. Good thing, considering it wasn't running. Blake would arrange for a mechanic to look at his car, but in the meantime, the truck was kind of cool. He remembered riding around with his grandfather around the farm as he fixed up fences. And he remembered the first time his grandfather let him help. His emotions now were mixed as compared to the day it happened. That was a big-boy day. Blake grinned to himself as he recalled feeling like he was all grown up.

Later, he realized it was just the beginning of what would turn out to be his worst nightmare. Farm chores. Hard, smelly, long hours of work. The scar on his arm was a constant reminder of one of his least favorites—milking the cows. Old Bessie had clocked him good with her hind leg when he'd squeezed too tight. It was also the beginning of his dreams to create a machine to do the work for him. Of course, somebody had already invented the automated milking machine, but his father had nixed the idea and every other idea Blake had suggested to make things easier. His father's old school ideas firmly set and unmovable.

Blake drove into town and parked down the street from the creamery, not wanting to use any customer parking spots. As he walked toward the building, visions surfaced, his brain in high design mode. A neon flashing light sign hanging above the doorway would be a great way to attract attention. Once people had ice cream on the brain, the craving would grow and turn into a sale. But you had to attract customers first, and the current sign did little to stand out. In fact, it blended.

People who passed by here every day would rarely even acknowledge the creamery existed. Unless something else caused them to want ice cream. Making a mental note, it would be one of the things he presented to the team. Although for Blake, it wasn't negotiable, he'd make sure they agreed.

He pushed open the door, the overhead bell jingling. Something it seemed every business in Hallbrook used to announce a customer's arrival. And something else that had room for improvement.

Zoe looked up at him and waved. "Good morning, Blake. You're right on time."

"Good morning. I'm a firm believer time is valuable for everyone and that lateness is rude. That was a concept drilled into me from the very beginning." He shot her a smile and then hung up his coat.

"Well, good. I see you took my advice about the jeans," she said, grinning.

Blake chuckled, moving around the counter to stand next to Zoe. "I'm not sure my dry cleaners would approve sticky stains on my suit."

"You're just in time to help me mix up a couple batches of ice cream. Grab an apron." She pointed to a row of them hanging on the wall by the door that led to the back room. "And then wash up. There's a larger sink in the back, but you can use the small one over there." She pointed next to one of the machines that looked like some kind of shake mixer. "There's soap and a hand towel in the cupboard below it."

"Thanks. I'll pass on the apron," he said, making his way to the sink. The jeans and sweater were a concession, but dressing like a woman? Not likely."

"Your choice, one you'll regret. I promise."

"I'll take my chances." He shrugged, drying off his hands and moving to stand next to her.

Two dimples appeared, Zoe's answering smile bright and cheerful. A feel-good smile. Just like the ice cream they sold at Peterson's. Interesting observation and way too mushy for his liking. "What's first, boss for the day?" Blake teased.

Her smile slipped a bit. "Well, first, I'd like to apologize for Scott's behavior. He's protective of me, and I think he's worried about you."

"Why would he be worried about me?" he asked.

"He saw you kiss me." Zoe shoved a bowl in his direction, her gaze fixated on something in front of her, almost as if she were intentionally trying not to look at him.

Blake winced. "Oh, that." That wasn't something he'd considered. He never dated women with children, so the thought process of private for a simple kiss was non-existent. Although the kiss wasn't simple. Not by any means. "I'm sorry. Did you set the record straight?"

"Of course. It was a birthday kiss, that's all. It's that since his dad left, it's just been him and me. I don't think he shares well, and I didn't remember to tell him until after dinner Saturday evening." Zoe dumped a few ingredients in her bowl and then shoved those in his direction also.

"No man is ever good enough for a boy's mother," he joked. "And for the record, we kissed, but in my opinion, the really good part was mutual." He leaned back against the counter and waited for instructions on what to do with the ingredients, but more than that, he wanted to hear her answer

"Do you want me to explain that to a nine-year-old boy?" Zoe turned to him, the frown on her face was not what he was hoping for.

He shook his head. "Good heavens, no. That was just to clear our air. I had to set Sarah straight as well, since you told her about us."

"Sarah?" she asked. "And there is no us."

"Well, Scott wasn't the only one who witnessed the kiss and commented. I got an earful from Sarah on the subject. She warned me off right and proper. Although I must say, she didn't give me any grief when she found out we had dinner together." The more he thought about it, the more it bothered him, Sarah's change in attitude all too convenient

"Wow. She hasn't said a thing to me about witnessing the err...*ummm*...kiss. I wonder why?" Zoe reached for more ingredients in the cupboard, placing them on the counter, but not before he saw a frown firmly etched on her face.

"Don't worry. I set her straight."

"We shouldn't have kissed like that. If Sarah and Scott noticed, there's no telling how many others in town have us getting hitched." She shook her head, an expression of mock horror on her face.

"Whoa. Slow down. I didn't say anything about getting married." Blake chuckled, but the word itself would have him running for the hills, or the city in his case, if he suspected she was right.

"I didn't say you. *Them.* And with us working together this week, tongues will surely wag. And Scott's got enough of an issue with everything without getting wind we're together. You know, as a couple." Zoe gripped the counter, the whites of her knuckles a good indicator of her tension and frustration with the situation.

"Our dinner last night didn't help, did it?" He hated to point it out and cause her more distress, but if what she said was true, there was a reality check they both needed to deal with.

"What's that mean?" she asked, the scowl on her face deepening.

"Plenty of folks saw us out together at Sally's. We both know it wasn't a date, but the people in town don't. What did you tell Sarah?"

"She asked about my night and felt bad canceling out. I told her you showed up and we all had dinner. To talk about the creamery and the contest. I thought I made it clear."

"Maybe not clear enough."

"What do you mean?" she asked.

"She grilled me about our date. Which it wasn't." Who was he trying to convince by repeating that fact—her or himself? Maybe both. "Sarah would hate it if I dated one of her friends; that's why she warned me off the night of your party. And it's the same reason I steered clear of you in high school." Now, why on earth would he tell her that? *Dumb move.* He was usually more polished and in control of his words, but not around Zoe it would seem.

"Wait, what?" she asked, her eyes wide as saucers.

"It's in the past, so I guess there's no harm in telling you now. I had a small crush on you." It was like letting go of a childhood secret, one he feared would make him look a fool.

Zoe laughed—really laughed. Not exactly the reaction he expected. "That must have been before the big crush you had on Tammy Wright. Most popular girl in school." She shook her head, grinning. She didn't believe him. Maybe it was better this way.

"It was." Blake wasn't about to tell her his crush on Tammy was to cure his crush on Zoe. She'd only laugh at him more, and it wouldn't accomplish a thing at this point. "I know what we should do."

"Do tell," she said dryly, trying to act all serious.

Blake would make this right. He was a master at fixing, and this was just one more escapade to extricate himself from. "Let's just make sure when people see us together, it's clear we aren't a couple. Prove to them what they saw and what they're thinking is all wrong."

"You mean go out of our way to not get along?" Zoe asked, her questioning expression not one of dismissal, at least not yet.

Blake nodded. "That would be a start. We'll wing it as we go along. Bitter adversaries in the contest or some such nonsense. In fact, it could be downright fun."

Zoe grinned, the change in her all too obvious as she relaxed. "I like it. We are adversaries, and there will only be one winner. It's believable, and since I'm hoping it will be me, I won't have to act very hard," she teased.

"Tell me something. I get it about the promotion and the raise. Why you'd want that, or why anyone would want it, is obvious. But I'm curious about the bonus money. What would you do with it?" Maybe he shouldn't have asked because it was getting personal and crossing lines, but he wanted to get to know her better. Even if they had just agreed to be adversaries. But while no one else was around, he was free to be himself with her.

"I've wanted to take Scott to Disney World for years, but I've never had the extra money to make his dream come true. We haven't gone on any vacations for that matter. I've scrimped and saved to make sure we have enough for the day-to-day living and tucked everything else away for emergencies. It would be nice after all these years of hard work to do something fun." Zoe used the back of her hand to brush her hair out of her face and pulled her bowl closer.

"I see." Knowing the truth made him regret she wouldn't get her dream if he got his. But this was business. Not to mention, it was *his* family.

"Time to get to work, mister. Here's the recipe for Maple-Walnut ice cream, my favorite flavor. Follow the directions and ask questions if you get stuck. I'll be right here beside you, mixing up a batch of Black Raspberry. Another one of my favorites."

"Sounds like you have lots of favorites." Blake chuckled before glancing down at the card he held. It was back to business and the time for introspection over. He was determined to prove he could do this. "Looks easy enough." *Not.* The instructions talked about hand-cranking and a salt and ice bath. Since when did ice cream require a bath? Another reason modern technology made sense.

"Try doing all twenty-six flavors. Some daily." She grinned, dumping a pile of ice into her bowl."

Blake frowned and shook his head. "I'm not sure I'd want to do this twenty-six times. Hey, aren't you going to measure?" he asked, picking up the bag of ice to follow her lead, finding it somewhat easier. Presumably, ice cream was made the same, just with twenty-six variations of ingredients.

"Don't worry. Usually, it's only a couple of batches a day, unless it's like the Fourth of July festival here in town. And no, I don't typically measure. I've done this so often I know what counts and what the quantity looks like by sight. You, on the other hand, must measure."

"Bossy much?" he mumbled under his breath, not wanting to get on her bad side.

"What's that?" she asked.

"Nothing. I'm just reading over the recipe."

Blake carefully measured out the ingredients Zoe had laid out for him while eying the hand-cranked wooden barrel he was expected to operate. An hour passed and he was on his final preparations, adding more maple syrup covered walnuts to the top of the semi-frozen concoction. Zoe had long since finished and cleaned up her mess and came to watch over him. "It's finished. I think."

Zoe nodded. "Nice. I should sample it before it goes in the freezer. Just to make sure we're offering a quality product to the customer. It's also one of my favorite parts of the job." She took a spoon and did a taste test. "*Hmmm*. That works. It's perhaps light on the nutty flavor, but it will be okay."

"Okay? I've never been one to settle for okay. I measured the walnuts exactly like the recipe called for. It can't be wrong."

She looked up at him, a smile on her face. "Was your measurement before or after you chopped them?"

Silly question. "Before."

Zoe nodded. "That's what I thought. You measure the nuts after their chopped. See," she said, pointing at the ingredients list on the index card. "The recipe calls for two cups of chopped nuts, not two cups of nuts chopped."

Forget silly. Now he was downright confused. "What's the difference?"

"About a half of a cup of nuts." She laughed. "Chopped nuts would mean the chopping comes first, then they're measured, nuts chopped—the chopping is after the nuts are measured. The order in which the words are listed makes a substantial difference. It's like that for all ingredients on recipes. Rookie mistake, but by the end of the week, you'll have this down pat." Zoe took the container from him and started toward the back room.

"Who said anything about all week? I only promised a day," he asked, forcing her to pause at the door and turn back.

"Your grandfather wants you to learn how to run the place. And it's my job to teach you. I can't do that in a single day."

This wasn't what he signed on for, although it did make sense. Partly for his grandfather's request, mostly because it meant he would be able to spend more one-on-one time with Zoe. "Fine. But only half days. I do have a renovation proposal to submit and my regular job to do."

"Fair enough. Remember, though, I've got a full-time job and a son, so your help will give *me* time to work on my proposal." Her smile was like a ray of sun on a rainy day.

"In that case, maybe I shouldn't help out," he teased.

"You wouldn't dare back out," she threatened, advancing toward him and picking up a handful of ice cubes along the way.

The doorbell jingled, announcing the arrival of a customer.

"Don't threaten me, or I'll have you fired," Blake said in a steely voice, glaring at her. He'd gone into an all-out adversarial mode with a switch of an internal button. Perfect timing as far as he was concerned.

"Oh dear, have I come at the wrong time? Are you not open yet?" The older woman stopped half way to the counter.

"We're open. Come on in," he said, turning to face the woman with a broad smile and his boyish charm. "Just a friendly discussion."

"If you say so," she said, looking back and forth between him and Zoe.

"It's all good, Mrs. Elliot. I've got your quart of lemon sherbet right here, and it's ready for pick-up." Zoe pulled it out from the freezer, rang up the order, and took the woman's money, her smile genuine.

"Thank you, dearie. You know, it may be none of my business, but you two need to get along, or it's going to be a couple of long weeks until the competition is over." The woman's suggestion was the confirmation his comment had worked. Soon, people all over town would know they were at each other's throats.

Zoe shook her head. "Everything's fine between us. I'm sorry you overheard Blake, but he isn't used to working in a kitchen. Don't you worry, his bark is worse than his bite." Zoe was going all out to play both sides of the discussion, leaving him to look like the bad guy.

"I reckon that's good then." She smiled and left the shop.

Zoe spun on her heels to face him the minute the door closed. "You wouldn't dare have me fired," she said, glaring at him, her hands on her hips.

This time it was Blake's turn to laugh at her. "I was only doing what we said we were going to do. Confuse the people in town and throw them off our scent."

"That was...oh. I get it." She shook her head. "Good thinking. Mrs. Elliot will be telling everyone we were fighting. You could have clued me in. I thought you were serious," she huffed.

"Contrary to what you believe about me, I'm not a mean guy, Zoe. I would never do anything to undermine what you do here, and you know it."

"Do I?" she asked, the lines of her forehead deepening.

Blake let out a breath of air. "You do if you trust your brain."

Zoe jerked her head toward the register. "I think I should teach you the basic skills of how to ring up an order and cash it out." She'd completely disregarded his subject, and the discussion was closed.

"Sounds like a plan." He finished wiping up the mess from the batch of ice cream he'd made and then joined her at the register.

By mid-morning, Blake knew the truth about what was really going on at Peterson's creamery. Zoe was overloaded with responsibility, and she was underpaid. He also knew being in close proximity to her was reviving some of his old feelings.

Feelings he'd long ago locked away. Zoe and Sarah had been best friends since kindergarten, but it hadn't been until she turned sixteen when Blake noticed her as more than a nuisance. She stopped being Sarah's best friend and had become a beautiful young woman.

It was also when he set his sights on Tammy, knowing he'd be overstepping his bounds to try and date his kid sister's best friend. The idea had been that Tammy would get Zoe off his brain. It worked, but that was then, and this was now. Unfortunately, Zoe wasn't the love 'em and leave 'em type of woman—but it was his.

Chapter Eight

WORKING WITH BLAKE WASN'T as bad as Zoe thought it would be. He didn't seem to mind getting sticky and dirty, and he didn't mind cleaning up the mess. She felt a little guilty using the opportunity to get him to do more than his fair share, and therefore, lightening her load. Chad and Henry arrived right at noon to start their shifts, giving Zoe a chance to do some paperwork and write down some ideas to go over with her team.

She'd set a meeting at four-thirty, in between the after school and dinner rushes. It would be a good time to get a jump-start on what everyone had found out over the weekend and to figure out which ideas were worth pursuing and which ones to let go. And hopefully, plenty of new suggestions to add to the growing pile. More was always good in the beginning.

Zoe frowned, the figures on the screen not adding up. Balancing the bank statement was one of her least favorite tasks, the multitude of ins and outs on the spreadsheet daunting.

Knock. Knock.

Zoe looked up, her office door opening even before she answered to reveal Sarah paying her a visit. She shoved the spreadsheet off to the side of her desk. "Hey, no-show," Zoe teased.

Her friend plopped into the chair opposite the desk and sat back. "Stop. I already apologized. Dalton needed me to do something for him and I couldn't say no."

"And let me guess...you had nothing to do with Blake showing up at Sally's."

Sarah shook her head, almost too adamantly for Zoe's liking. "Of course not. I heard you two had a date. Of course, after that kiss at your party, it's no wonder. The kiss you somehow never mentioned. I kept waiting for you to tell me."

"Knock it off. First off, it was a birthday kiss. Don't get all crazy on me about it. It's bad enough

Scott saw it, and now, he's a little perturbed. With Blake." Why did everyone want to make such a big deal about it? *Because it was a crazy good kiss.*

"If he saw what I saw, it's no wonder. You two were all into that kiss. Half the town saw it by the time you were through."

"Half the town wasn't there," Zoe countered.

"So, half the people at the party." Her friend laughed, not at all backing down.

"Just want you to get your facts straight," Zoe teased, hoping to bring the conversation to a natural end and find out why Sarah was here. The books were calling her name.

"You've always liked him, but then I thought you outgrew the crush. Am I wrong?" Sarah questioned, not letting it go.

"I didn't realize you knew," Zoe answered without thinking it through. It was an admission of sorts and one that couldn't possibly be misunderstood.

Sarah leaned forward, putting her elbows on the desk. "Of course I knew. I'm your best friend."

"Why didn't you say anything?" Zoe asked.

"Because I didn't want it to happen. I saw it as just plain wrong." Sarah winced. "At least it was when we were younger. I wasn't about to let my big brother steal my bestie."

Zoe shook her head, surprised at her friend's declaration. "Sarah, you know it wouldn't have been that way. We're like sisters. Nothing comes between us. Ever."

"Well, I was sixteen, and that's what I was afraid of back then. I was a kid. But what about now? You still like him, don't you?" Sarah was persistent, but Zoe wasn't willing to give her anything that would push her along into thinking there were any residual feelings.

"Not in the same way. I promise. It was a long time ago. I'm different now, and I've got a son to consider."

"Then why the dinner date? You invited him to join you," Sarah said, her direct gaze never wavering.

"It wasn't a date. And if I'm not wrong, I'm a little worried you set the whole thing up. Come on, Sarah, fess up. You canceled and sent Blake there, didn't you?"

"Oh no, I had nothing to do with Blake going to Sally's," Sarah insisted. Almost a little too forcefully for Zoe's liking. It reminded her of a child trying to talk their way out of trouble.

"Arghhh. It wasn't a date. Just two friends sharing a meal. Blake had a series of mishaps and his date canceled out on him when he informed her he'd be seriously late. The type of women he dates and the person I am, operate on two different levels. Fast and slow. And Blake doesn't do anything slow." She'd seen it in action with Tammy in high school and had been kept abreast of his comings and goings through the many tales of Sarah.

"I'm glad his first date fell through. I didn't like Tracy the last time I met her. And after I saw him kiss you at the party, I realized the two of you deserve a shot at being together." Her friend's declaration was surprising.

Zoe frowned. *A shot at* being together. No. No. No. "Sarah...tell me the truth. What did you do?"

"Nothing." Which meant something, her friend's short answer more telling than her earlier denial.

"Sarah...start talking."

"Okay, so nothing much anyway. Let's just say when the mechanic looks at his Porsche, there won't be anything wrong with it," Sarah admitted, not a trace of guilt in her expression.

"You didn't mess with his car. Please, tell me you didn't." Blake would be furious if he found out. Zoe's shock level left her reeling and too rattled to be angry. Sarah had overstepped her bounds.

"I did. I only pulled the starter coil. I feel like I kept you two apart in high school. Now that I'm older, I think it would be cool if you were my sister-in-law. We're like sisters anyway," Sarah said by way of excuse.

It worked, at least with Zoe. She didn't think Blake would be so forgiving. "Will you listen to yourself? Don't let anyone hear you talking like that. We're busy trying to squash the rumors."

"What rumors? And who's we?" Sarah asked, not at all put off by her admission.

Zoe let out a deep breath. "Blake and I."

"So, I'm right. Do tell," she insisted.

Zoe shook her head. There was no making Sarah understand, but she'd try, for Blake's sake. "Your grandfather has him working here at the creamery. I figured you knew that too. We decided to make sure the people in town don't go getting any ideas.

Ideas like you seem to have." She had to make Sarah understand the reality of the situation and to nix any crazy notions she might come up with. How could she mess with his car? For that matter, how did she know what to do?

Dalton. Her new boyfriend, the auto mechanic.

"What exactly are you doing about it?" her friend asked.

Zoe remembered when Blake had threatened her. It wasn't her finest moment because she'd actually believed him. Normally, she was a little quicker on the uptake, but where Blake was concerned, it would seem her radar shorted out. "Blake picked a fight and yelled at me when a customer walked in. It was quite a sight. Although..." Zoe shook her head and shrugged. "It would have been nice if I'd known in advance what he was going to do. I thought he was serious and wanted to have me fired."

"Sounds like foreplay to dating. Just saying," Sarah teased.

"Stop. It's not that way. I'm older and over your brother. Trust me."

"If you say so, but if you get a chance to kiss again—I think you should. Maybe then you'll start to understand what I see." Her friend was incorrigible. And unfortunately, the image of Blake kissing her again was something she'd considered. But that was something she'd keep to herself. "We're competitors in this contest, and I need to win. And you're going to help me with the renovations."

"Renovations?" Sarah frowned.

"To redesign the creamery."

"Ummm, you're forgetting one thing."

"What's that?" Zoe asked, knowing that whatever it was, she'd talk Sarah out of her objections. She needed her help. Sarah knew her grandfather and Zoe needed to tap into that knowledge.

"My brother *is* the other team. I really don't want to be dragged into this contest on either side."

As if she'd forget that fact. Not remotely possible given the situation. "Too bad. I need you here to come up with some ideas for team Zoe. As my best friend, you're expected to help me out. Just think, if I win, I can take Scott to Disney World. And you could come with us, based on how much the prize money is. How's that for incentive?" Zoe hadn't given it much thought before, but it would be fun.

The two of them hadn't done anything together of that magnitude since high school.

"Well, now you're talking. Disney World or Blake? I'll take Disney World." Sarah laughed.

Zoe let out a sigh of relief. Her unofficial fifth member on the team. "Great. The group is meeting here today at four-thirty."

"Gotcha. I've got some things to do before then. See you later," Sarah said, jumping to her feet.

"Bye. Four-thirty. Don't forget."

Sarah waved and pulled open the door to leave. Blake stood there, ready to knock. It was like Grand Central Station in her office today.

"I was just coming to make sure everything was okay in here," Blake spoke first, not at all surprised to find his sister in her office.

It was sweet of him to check up on Zoe. "Yes. Sarah's just leaving."

Her friend waved and sailed past Blake. "Later, brother dearest."

Zoe shook her head. "I had to set her straight again about our dinner together." Zoe wouldn't tell him it was Sarah who had a hand in ending his date Saturday night. Or that she suspected his sister had a hand in them being at the same place and at the same time. Not that Sarah had fessed up. *Yet*.

"Great. Ummm, we could use you out here. I'm not that much help at this point." Blake grinned, setting her heart to racing.

She shoved aside the direction her thoughts were drifting and tried to concentrate. "Why, are we that busy?" she asked, glancing at her watch.

"Yes. Sorry."

"Busy is good. It keeps me employed." Zoe laughed as she stood and followed him to the front. Zoe stepped in and managed the register, letting the others focus on taking orders and filling them. The rush lasted about an hour, but it was enough to put an end to her office work. It wouldn't be long before the others showed up for the team meeting.

Watching Blake in action had been eye-opening. The guy was friendly with every customer; like he was born to serve and make others happy. The precision he used when making desserts or even putting a scoop of ice cream on a cone was that of a perfectionist. And he was a flirt. Blake Peterson wasn't a dine-and-dash guy like she'd accused him of being. Instead, he was a love-and-dash guy.

With Scott to consider, even though part of her wanted to let her hair down and have some fun as friends with Blake, she couldn't. Scott was far too impressionable, and he'd been hurt enough when his dad walked out. Zoe wouldn't let it happen again, and Blake would be leaving, sooner rather than later.

Chapter Nine

♥

THE NEXT COUPLE OF days flew by for Zoe, or at least the afternoons when Blake showed up, they did. The rest, not so much. Mornings she was busy keeping up with the financial accounting and bank books, as well as the hundred other details of running the place. And nights, well those were another matter entirely.

Scott wasn't overly thrilled about Blake being at the creamery a lot and was finding it difficult to understand why he had to work with her if they were competitors. Not an easy thing to explain to a nine-year-old who didn't like the guy—seeing him as a threat to Scott's time with his mother.

By Wednesday, they'd fallen into a routine at the creamery that worked well. Blake helped out on the floor, and the bonus of his helping gave her the ability to leave on time every day and go home to work on her designs.

She stepped out of the office and paused when she heard loud voices. Zoe peeked through the windowed door that separated the back rooms from the front shop and was surprised not to see any customers. The employees, however, were in a heated debate, and Blake was right in the mix.

Curiosity piqued, she slipped into her assistant-manager role and pushed open the door to join the group. "What's going on? Doesn't look like any work is getting done, and you all standing around arguing about something won't be good if a customer walks in."

Everyone stopped talking and turned, all eyes on her. No one looked upset or flustered or anything for that matter.

"We were just having a friendly discussion. Don't get all bent out of shape," Blake teased, his smile firmly in place. Some of the tension ebbed out, but not all of it.

"It didn't sound friendly from where I stood," she countered.

"Sorry, Zoe. We were discussing the competition. Each side has its own definite views, and we were comparing notes," Lindsey spoke up, trying to clear the air.

Zoe had no problem with them discussing the contest as long as it didn't interfere with their work, and by the looks of things with no customers, they were in the clear. "Okay. Thanks. Just watch for customers so we don't run them off with our little contest."

"It's a little more than a simple discussion," Blake offered, a gleam in his eyes she'd quickly learned meant he was up to something. "The staff thinks the contest is too long and drawn out. Chad came up with the idea of an ice cream challenge between employees. Just for fun, of course." There was nothing wrong with fun but she needed to hear more before she agreed.

"An ice cream challenge?" she asked.

"Yes. Like who can eat a dish of ice cream the fastest without brain freeze," Chad said, the kid in him coming out. He was one of the high schoolers who worked part-time, but who was also a reliable and talented worker.

"They figured a friendly challenge will help keep the peace until this is over. Keep things fun," Blake explained, taking a couple of steps in her direction.

"Sounds okay to me. Have fun," Zoe said, turning back toward her office and keeping a safe distance from Blake. She'd discovered it was the best way not to think about him as often.

"Not so fast, Zoe. You work here, too," Blake chided.

"I don't think—"

"But you have to join in to make it fair. Team Blake has three members represented, and now that Tony's here, we would have three people from Team Zoe. A mini competition of sorts," Lindsey pleaded the cause, excitement shining in her eyes.

Zoe wondered if it had more to do with Chad than the ice cream challenge. She was pretty sure the girl had a crush on him. "Fine. Do we get to pick our own flavor?"

"I think that's only fair," Blake said, the others nodding in agreement.

"Let's make this quick while there aren't customers, and if someone comes in, we stop immediately. The customer always comes first." Zoe wasn't against having a little fun, but she had to set some parameters. Not only to keep the whole situation under control, but also to maintain her position of authority as boss. It wouldn't do to start acting like besties and get all chummy with the staff.

"Yes, Ms. Carruthers," Brenda spoke up. She was a shy girl, which is what had drawn Zoe to hire her in the first place. A reliable employee, but obviously working here was giving her more confidence if she was able to join in the group fun.

Each person put two scoops of ice cream in a cup, Zoe choosing her favorite—Maple Walnut. She couldn't help but notice Blake chose the same flavor as she did, leaving her to wonder why. She'd ask him later, but not in front of the group. They all compared the size of their scoops to make sure it was fair. The six of them formed a circle, a spoon in one hand and their cup of ice cream in the other.

"Get ready," Chad said, watching everyone intently to make sure no one got a head start. "On your mark, get set, go."

Zoe dug in avidly like the rest of them, each one determined to win. The competitive spirit was alive and well in this group. Spoonful after spoonful, she shoveled the sweet, creamy ice cream in her mouth. On second thought, she shouldn't have chosen something with nuts, the process of chewing them slowing her down. It just meant taking bigger bites.

Glancing at the others, she noted Blake was almost done. There was no way she wanted to lose to him. Taking the last of her second scoop, a bite three times the size of her normal intake, she shoved it in her mouth. And held up her bowl. "Mmmm, mmmm," she said, her mouth full as she gestured to her empty bowl.

"Great job, Zoe," Lindsey said, smiling. "Woohoo! Team Zoe wins."

"She has to swallow it," Chad called out, shoveling another bite in his mouth.

Zoe swallowed. Her hand flew to her head, the sudden pain stinging.

"Brain freeze," Chad cried out, laughing.

"Done," Blake said, the cocky grin on his face meant for her as he declared himself the winner.

"Fine. You win," Zoe acknowledged, her head still throbbing. "It was fun, but not the brain freeze. Next time think of something better. Blake has a bigger mouth, so he had an unfair advantage," she teased.

"Says who?" he asked, acting offended. "I won fair and square."

Zoe grinned. "Says me."

"You would know," Blake quipped, using her opening to get back at her. The teasing light in his eyes brought the memory of their kiss flaming back to life. She'd tried to put it out of her head, but with three little words, it was back, center and front.

"Whatever." Zoe shrugged, rinsing out her bowl and putting it in the dishwasher. "I've got to get back to work."

The front door opened, and a couple of kids came in. The after-school crowd was starting to arrive. She headed for the back office, where she stayed, spending some of the time to work on her designs. Her team's research was paying off, and she was pleased with the progress they were making. Now, if only she could stop thinking about the opposite team's leader.

Knock. Knock.

Lost in thought, the sound startled her. Expecting one of the staff coming back to let her know they needed help, she was surprised to see Blake standing there with a spoon in one hand and a bowl in the other.

"I would have thought you'd have left by now," Zoe said, glancing at her watch and then back at him.

"Normally, yes. But I decided to try my hand again at making a batch of Maple Walnut ice cream since you found me lacking on my first attempt."

"It wasn't bad. That's what we ate today." She laughed.

"Try this," he offered, stepping forward and closing the distance between them. He scooped out a bite and held it out to her.

Zoe stood up, taking his hand to guide it to her mouth. The warmth of the contact between them sent shivers down her spine. *Get a grip.* "Mmmm, much better. I'd say almost perfect."

"Almost?" He frowned. He used the second spoon he'd brought with him to scoop out another spoonful, this time eating it himself. "I'd say perfection."

"I take it Maple Walnut is your favorite, and that's your expert opinion," she teased, remembering his choice for the contest and trying to find out why he picked that particular flavor. Not that she wanted it to be because she'd picked it, but because she was simply curious.

"Not at all. I'm more of a Coffee fan. The bolder, the better." His answer surprised her.

"Then why did you pick Maple Walnut today? We have Coffee ice cream." Zoe waited, not sure how she wanted him to answer.

"I know." He shrugged. "I picked it because I made it. Can't think of a better reason than that, can you?" he asked, grinning. The man was incorrigible—and a flirt.

"Ha-ha. You can wipe that silly grin off your face, mister, considering you're decorated with ice cream."

Blake used his hand to swipe at his mouth. "It was a big bite. You know, for my big mouth," he teased, recalling her earlier comment.

"Sorry about that. I thought it was good for our don't-get-along message. And you missed." Zoe reached up, and using her thumb, swiped at the corner of his mouth." Her gaze locked with his as if time had stopped. "All gone," she mumbled.

Blake grabbed her hand to keep her from stepping away. He drew her close, his mouth landing on hers. Heaven-sent kisses were his specialty, and this one tasted like Maple Walnut—her favorite.

The kiss or the ice cream, she was no longer sure. Maybe it was the combination of both.

"Thank you," he murmured when he drew back. "I've got to clean up and head for an appointment. I'm glad you approve of my efforts this time." With that, he turned and left.

The problem was she approved of all his efforts. Too much, in fact. Her fingertips touched her lips, the feel of his mouth still on hers. Zoe knew Blake was a good guy, and his tender side, kindness, determination to succeed, and outgoing qualities all appealed to her. Her old school crush was clearly rekindled. What was there not to crush on?

His fast pace motto with regards to love and life—that's what. Something she couldn't let herself forget.

Chapter Ten

♥

BLAKE RESISTED THE URGE to head to the creamery Saturday morning, choosing instead to work on one of the projects that he'd been hired to design. The company wanted a more efficient way of building multiple sizes of the same window. Not exactly exciting, but he still enjoyed the challenge of designing something to fit the customer's needs.

Currently, each window size required changes on the machine, which meant downtime. Productivity would increase almost fivefold by the time he was finished. No lost jobs, just more efficiency based on high technology. It was no different than he was trying to do for the creamery and the Peterson dairy farm.

By lunch, he hadn't accomplished much, other than to think about what prompted the second kiss he'd delivered to Zoe. She wasn't immune to his kisses, her sudden response the reason he'd pulled away. It wouldn't do to give her the wrong impression. Although how she *couldn't* get the wrong idea was beyond him. He was sending out mixed signals, but it was as if his brain had a mind of its own, and it was overruling the commonsense side he trusted.

So much so, by the time he was ready to head over to the creamery, he had an alternate plan in place. One that wouldn't have him going to the creamery at all today. Spending more time with Zoe would be far more effective at getting her out of his system. Now, all he had to do was convince her to agree. Blake hit the speed dial to call Zoe at the shop, knowing she would still be there.

"Peterson's Ice Creamery. How can I help you?" an employee answered, his business voice professional and courteous.

"Hey, this is Blake. I'm looking for Zoe. Is she still there?"

"Sure is. Hang on." A loud crackle had him pulling the phone away from his ear, the noise sounding like the phone crashing to the counter.

"Hey, Blake. What's up? I thought you'd be here by now," Zoe said in a rush.

"I was going to come in, but I've got a better idea. One that involves you." It was time to work his persuasive magic.

"Oh, what's that? she asked, the surprise in her voice not unexpected. It would be the first, and hopefully, the last time he would be asking her to partner up with him for a journey.

"Well, I know it's been hectic at the creamery with the added stress of trying to pull together the designs. We only have another week before we submit, but I had an idea that I think you'll really like. What if I showed you what I'm aiming for in the contest designs, and then perhaps it would give you a better understanding of what I'm trying to accomplish so you don't see me as the bad guy in all of this."

"It's not hard to picture a polished, high speed, stainless-steel environment," Zoe teased, the sound of her laughter making him smile.

The only problem, though, was that the image she perceived was not at all the way the creamery would look. It was more than stainless steel, and for some reason, he was determined to show her. Wanted to share his visions with her and get her opinion. "New is always good. In life, work, relationships—everything. It keeps things exciting and never boring. The nostalgia approach is the same old same old and inevitably becomes boring. It's not just stainless steel and efficiency as one steps into the future, and I want to prove it."

"*Hmmm.* So, if I were interested, which I'm not saying I am, but what do you have in mind for this lesson of show and tell?" she asked.

"I want to take you to a place in the city, let you see, hear, and feel the difference." More importantly, a way for him to spend time with her to realize she would eventually bore him the same way all women eventually did.

"Are you asking me on a date?" Zoe asked, her voice wary. She was serious. Something he'd have to fix.

"No, consider it a casual business meeting." It would also allow Blake to stop in at his place and pick up a few things, but he sensed it was better to keep her focused on the business aspect of the arrangement.

"I see. So, are we talking about Lancaster?"

"Actually, I was thinking of New York City. I know the best place to take you."

"But that's hours away," she said. Judging by her voice, she was frowning on the other end of the line. A frown he'd kiss away if they were in the same room.

"Not by helicopter." Blake was second-guessing his own motive. What he couldn't understand was the effect Zoe had on his brain.

"Oh. I see. It's a nice offer, but I'm afraid I can't go," she said, surprising him. He couldn't think of any of his female acquaintances who would turn down the offer.

An idea suddenly occurred to him. "Are you afraid of the helicopter or me?" he asked, trying to figure out her reasoning in order to overcome it.

"Neither. Well, maybe a little of the helicopter as I've never been in one before. The issue is that I'm done my shift in half an hour and due to pick Scott up from Devon's house."

The kid would be the perfect fodder to squash any of his reckless impulses. "Bring him. There's plenty of room."

"I'm not sure that's a good idea, considering how he feels about you and all. It was a little rough at the diner with his surly attitude toward you. I'm not looking for a repeat performance."

She had a point, but Blake didn't mind Scott. He understood the boy's protective streak and considered it a valuable quality in the young man. "This would be a chance for him to see us together as friends; maybe it would reassure him."

Zoe let out a deep breath. "I'm not so sure of that, but it's nice to know you consider us friends."

"Of course I do. You're Sarah's best friend and we get along quite well. Other than our differing views on the creamery renovations, that is." There had to plenty of things about her that would irritate him, he just had to look harder than most to find them when it came to Zoe.

"I tell you what. Let me pick Scott up from the Parker's, and then I'll text you if he's interested." At least she wasn't telling him no.

"Are you kidding? No matter how much he hates me, he'll want to fly in a helicopter," Blake said, chuckling. Zoe wouldn't be able to say no once she told Scott.

"You're probably right."

"Meet me here at Peterson's Airfield and I'll have the chopper ready to go." It wouldn't take him that long to prepare everything, but he did need to let Hank out to run before putting him on lockdown for the rest of the afternoon until he got home. Asking his father was out of the question because there would always be conditions tied to anything he offered to help with.

"*Ummm*, you're flying it?"

"Yes," Blake said, laughing. "I've got my license and at least five hours of experience on my own," he teased.

"*Ummm*, please tell me you're joking," she said, her voice barely a whisper.

"I'm joking. I've logged over a thousand hours and haven't lost anyone yet. In the city, it's way more efficient way for getting around to the companies I need to visit. My clients are from all over the country."

"Okay, then," He could tell she wasn't convinced, but at least she'd agreed. That's what mattered. "I'll text you when I pick up Scott to confirm or cancel. It's the best I can promise." So it was a maybe, which was still better than a no.

"Gotcha." They hung up, and Blake slid in his car, hoping it would start. The mechanic hadn't found anything wrong with it, the darn thing starting right up for him. So now it was a waiting game to see if it acted up again. The mechanic had given him the look he hated—the one that said *are you sure you had the clutch in*? His *inner-not-so-confident* self, wondered if it was true, not that he'd admit it. Instead, he'd smoothly laughed it off with a joke.

Today, it started right away, the smooth sound of the engine pleasing. Fast and powerful, just the way Blake liked things. Another reason he enjoyed the helicopter as a means of transportation.

Thirty minutes later, a text notification vibrated on his phone.

Zoe: On our way.

Blake: Told you.

He couldn't resist sending the response. Scott may not like him, but his helicopter was another story. After finishing all the preparations, he was gassed up and ready to go. He drove back to the house to let Hank out for a run.

Opening the front door, the dog came running. *Woof. Woof.*

Blake bent down to pet him. "Yes, I know you want out. Go do your business. I'll be gone a couple of hours."

The dog took off running toward the meadow, looking for fresh sights and scents. He hoped the silly dog didn't roll in the manure or he'd have to be locked in the barn until Blake got back from the trip.

It wasn't long before Zoe pulled up in her car. Scott got out and glanced in Zoe's direction before looking back at him.

"Where's the helicopter? I don't see one," Scott said, his attitude leaving a bit to be desired.

"At the airfield. We'll ride over in the truck."

"Whatever." The boy was noncommittal, but that was sure to vanish when he was strapped in the big whirlybird and sky-bound.

"Hey, Zoe. Glad you both could make it."

Woof. Woof. Hank came bounding toward them, something Blake had to stop, knowing the dog's penchant for jumping on people to say hello. It was a bad habit he hadn't been able to break. He moved forward to block the dog's approach.

Too late, Hank went around him and jumped.

On Zoe. She squealed in surprise, putting her hands up to block the dog's exuberant hello.

Blake winced. "I'm sorry," he said, reaching for Hank.

"He's fine." To his astonishment, Zoe got the dog under control and was petting him, Hank lapping up the attention.

Scott moved forward to pet the dog, and Hank licked his face. The kid laughed. "You're a good boy, aren't you?" he asked, hugging the dog's neck.

Blake shook his head in wonder. The kid had no hang-ups about his dog. "Meet Hank. Sorry for the rude introduction. He gets excited around new people and it's his way of saying hello. He sort of came with the bad habit, one I've never been able to eradicate."

Zoe scratched Hank behind his ears, the dog shifting his head around for her to get at a better angle. "He's fine. Dogs get excited, just like people."

"Yeah, but people don't jump on you," Blake said, not about to excuse the behavior issue.

"True," she said, nodding. "I didn't know you had a dog. He's such a cutie pie."

"I found him on the side of the road a few years back and we've been pals ever since."

"That's shocking. I didn't think you liked anything permanent in your life and having a pet is a committed relationship," she teased, her smile taking the sting out of her words.

Unfortunately, she was right. It just didn't sound good coming from her as an assessment of his life. "True. I never thought of it that way. He's a good listener, which makes up for any other shortcomings he may have."

Zoe's eyebrows rose a notch in disbelief. Okay, so maybe admitting he talked to his dog a lot by way of discussions wasn't the smartest of ideas. So much for the confident, cocky attitude he liked to portray. Now, she'd see him as an old softie.

Scott and Hank had taken off and were chasing each other through the yard, the boy laughing. "I think we should bring Hank with us." He nodded toward the pair in the front yard, watching them play, a carefree look on Scott's face. It was clear the boy was smitten with Hank.

"He loves dogs. I don't have time for one, but he's always begging me to change my mind. It couldn't hurt. The flight to the city might be rosier, that's for sure." Her eyes twinkled with merriment.

"Consider it done." Blake whistled, and the dog came running, a sullen Scott right behind him. "Hey, Scott, how would you like to ride with Hank in the back seat of the chopper?"

The kid's eyes lit up. "Sure, that sounds great. I mean, that's cool." He tried hard to school his features but wasn't having any luck.

"And if it's okay with your mother, you can both ride in the back of the truck to the airfield. We're just following the dirt road down the property line that leads there. Scott can hold Hank's leash." Blake looked at Zoe for permission.

Zoe shrugged. "I guess he can. If you're sure it's safe."

"I promise they'll both be fine. It's not far from here."

They all got in the truck, and Blake drove over to the airstrip, going extra slow and keeping a close watch on Scott and Hank in the back. Not that he needed to; Zoe was doing a good job of keeping watch on her own. It seemed as though the pair were in their own world, Scott's arm around Hank, the two in a deep discussion of some sort. The wind and the glass divider kept Blake in ignorance, but the animated look on his face spoke volumes.

Blake pulled up to the building and got out, lowering the tailgate for the boy and his new best friend to hop down. They all walked toward the chopper, Scott keeping his eyes glued on the machine.

"Pretty cool, huh?" Blake asked, sensing Scott's attitude toward him was changing.

"It's okay, I guess." The kid shrugged, but wide eyes the size of saucers gave away his true emotion.

Blake helped them inside, strapping the harnesses and checking them twice. Including Zoe's, which was a little more difficult as she tried to help, their hands tangling up together. Her hair against the back of his hand was like silk, and her scent, fresh and citrusy, making him want to drink in more of the country freshness.

This was supposed to be a lesson in moving past his desire to spend time with Zoe, not increase the need. Hank's over-the-top greeting should have been enough to parallel her with the few other women he'd brought to meet his dog, but it didn't, her reaction surprising. It made him realize even more, that perhaps the reason Zoe didn't match up with the other women he'd taken out, was because she *was* different. Lumping her in their category was obviously a mistake.

He flipped a few of the switches, powered up the blades, and then rechecked the gauges making sure everything was perfect on his checklist before take-off. It was also a good way to quit thinking about the woman sitting next to him.

"We're just about ready to take off," he said, pushing the shifter forward to increase the speed of the blades. The chopper vibrated with the intensity, the whirring sound growing louder and louder, ending the ability to hear without the use of the headsets. He flipped another switch to turn them on. The chopper started to lift and soon they were in the air and headed for the city. "Everyone okay?" he asked.

"I'm good," Zoe said, her voice sounding strained, but it was a good sign she had her face pressed to the glass and was looking down.

"This is cool," Scott said, grinning, one arm wrapped around Hank. The boy's dislike of Blake was long forgotten—or at least for the moment, it was. And a trip to Candy Bar Mountain should seal the deal.

Chapter Eleven

♥

THE HELICOPTER RIDE HAD been unnerving for Zoe, but her son's enthusiasm and Hank's gentle hand licks of reassurance calmed her nerves. It was as if the dog had sensed her distress and wanted to help. Once they touched down at the helipad at LaGuardia airport, her racing heart had finally settled back into a normal rhythm. Like clockwork, a limousine arrived, and they were all driven to Blake's special place – a candy shop of all things.

Candy Bar Mountain.

It had a nostalgic ring to the name, but that's where nostalgia stopped. Inside, the place was a madhouse. Kids dashing every which way, machines whirring and clanging, and the colors—wow. Every color imaginable was in sight. A high-speed train raced around at the top of the walls close to the ceiling, making imaginary stops at each chocolate mountain. Futuristic contemporary was the words that came to her to describe the place. It was like watching the Jetsons when she was a kid. High tech, futuristic color, and craziness all around.

The noise level had to be comparable to a sports game in a closed stadium or a rock concert. There were children, lots of them. Crying children. Happy children. And everything in between. Scott was in the happy children category. Any reservations he had about Blake vanished.

It was no wonder Blake left Hank with a friend at the airport; a dog wouldn't be allowed through the front door. Everywhere she looked, the place with teaming with employees dressed in starchy, clean aprons as they hurried about waiting on customers and topping off the automatic dispenser machines.

Gleaming white ceramic tile floors and display upon display designed to attract and tempt a child into insisting they have one of whatever was for sale. Boxes that looked like Christmas packages were loaded with chocolates and cookies and gin-gerbread. Tin cans with every flavor of popcorn imaginable. Hot chocolate machines spun out plenty of dark, rich cocoa to the customers. A drawing card sure to ramp up even the sourest child, at least until they came down from the sugar high.

"Mom, can I go look around. Please?" Scott asked.

"Only if you promise to look and not touch," she said, knowing full well she had about zero chance of reining him in.

Scott took off like a flash, moving to stand next to some children watching a candy machine churn out taffy. Long, ooey-gooey strips of red thick sugar balls were stretched and restretched until it was ready for packaging.

"This is crazy," she said, turning to Blake. There was activity going on everywhere she looked.

"Crazy good, right? Can't you feel the energy and the excitement? The lines at the register are non-stop, which makes for a good bottom line.

"I don't know. I like the more laid-back candy shops. The ones where you feel like you were at a five and dime store. This is just overwhelming." There was no peace or time to enjoy. It was rush, rush, rush. Zoe operated at a much slower speed.

"But profitable." Blake frowned, not understanding her point. "I mean, look at this." He led her to an area with a table. "Acrylic seats and tables. No wear. No tear. Just sanitize, and it's ready for the next person to enjoy an ice cream soda."

"If they can get comfortable. Talk about hard as rock candy." She grinned at her own joke, pleased she come up with one. It normally wasn't her forte. "Everything is just so colorful and yet impersonal. It reminds me of Willie Wonka's chocolate factory but without Willie Wonka and the Oompa-Loompas. I'm surprised they don't have a travel machine that runs on fizzy soda." Zoe was on a roll.

"Maybe I should suggest it to them." Blake smiled at her, a really topsy-turvy wonderful smile. "That was one of my favorite movies when I was a kid."

"Mine, too. What do you know? Maybe we should watch it together at my place. Having Scott around makes it officially not dork-city for adults. Besides, maybe it will remind you of the old times and how wonderful they can be. You do remember it was Charlie, the sweet Bland kind boy who won after he bought his ticket at a five and dime store—not a high-tech sweet shop. That was more Violet's style."

"Wow, you remember all that?" he asked, nodding in amazement.

Zoe laughed. "Absolutely. I watched it over and over."

"Can I buy you a shake so you can try out the rock candy table?" Blake asked, using her own description of the table to tease. His grin made the offer and the man irresistible.

"Sure," she said, glancing up at the menu board on the wall. Even that was on a rotating spindle. Read fast or just name something—it was sure to be there somewhere. "There must be a hundred flavors. How does anyone choose?"

Blake turned to face her. "Name your favorite candy."

"Okay, then. I choose butterscotch."

"One butterscotch shake coming up. Watch this. Press a button and voila! The machine makes it. Programmable machines simplify and speed up the process," he said, handing her the drink.

"But you missed all the fun of watching the soda jerk make it." She never cared for the term, but it was the old-fashioned frame of reference. She was glad the word server was used now because she would have liked being referred to as a soda jerk. It would have been enough for her to change jobs.

"You won't win this one with me. I love the action. So many choices. What's Scott's favorite?" Blake asked.

That was easy. "Root beer barrels. He's addicted to the things."

"One root beer float coming right up." Blake punched a few buttons, swiped his card to pay, and then stepped back to wait. "He likes the name. I did when I was younger, at least until I found out it wasn't actually a beer." Blake chuckled, the float pouring out through the dispenser into the automatically dropped cup within thirty seconds.

Zoe shook her head. Surely, he was joking. "That's terrible. I hope you're wrong about Scott. I'll go get him and meet you back here at the table area." She moved off, intent on finding her son and hoping he was keeping his promise. After making two turns around the store, she finally found him—with Blake.

"He wandered up and I gave him the shake. Seems like he's an all-American boy with the same idea as the rest of us guys." Blake's I-told-you-so grin was telling.

She frowned. "You mean—"

"Yes. Blake shot her a wink, knowing she wouldn't be happy with his answer. Zoe chalked it up to a boys-will-be-boys thing. Not to mention, she was thrilled the two of them were finally getting along. It would seem her son's favor could be bought with some doggy love, boy toys offering fun and adventure, and of course—sugar.

"Isn't this place cool, mom?" Scott asked.

"Maybe to some. It's like a flash in time that will be over as soon as the sugar rush ends. Memories aren't created in places like this." Just like the helicopter was a flash of wealth and a reminder of why they weren't suited. Which was a problem since her crush was fast becoming more than that. Even with their differences, she couldn't help but respect Blake, and like him, for the lack of a better word.

"I won't forget it. *Ever.* I've asked Blake to bring me back here and he said yes," her son said, beaming up at Blake. This was a new twist and not one that would help her situation. Giving in to her attraction would lead to heartache, and she'd had enough of that when Larry deserted her. Poor Scott would be in for a hard let down when Blake did a disappearing act and left Hallbrook.

"Sorry, I was going to tell you, but he beat me to it. I hope that was okay." Blake had the good graces to look apologetic even though it wouldn't do a thing when it came to dealing with Scott down the road.

"You shouldn't make promises you can't keep," she offered, using a gentle voice to make her comment come across lighter than the words portrayed. It was something Larry had done to Scott all the time.

"What's that supposed to mean?" he asked, frowning. So much for light, the message he'd received was more of a set down and he'd taken offense.

Zoe struggled for the words to explain. "When the contest is over, you'll be long gone. Back here—to the city you love."

"Unless I win. Then I'd be sticking around a bit to oversee the renovations. And then there's always the offside chance my grandfather will let me pitch my other ideas for the company."

"Like I said, when the contest is over, you'll be long gone. I don't intend to lose." She couldn't lose. There was too much at stake, and she refused to think of the alternatives to winning. An alternative which would have her looking for a new job.

Blake shook his head. "You don't give up, do you?"

"Nope. And I've got an idea. Tomorrow, it'll be my turn to show you what I'm trying to accomplish with *my* designs, and hopefully, it will awaken some good memories of what it's like to step back in time and slow down." The idea popped into her head and stuck. Bringing her here hadn't changed Zoe's impressions one bit, but perhaps the same wouldn't be said about Blake after tomorrow. *If he agreed.* She waited as he thought her offer through.

"I'm game.," he said, nodding.

She swallowed hard after a big gulp of her sundae, forgetting the potential brain freeze. Luckily, it didn't happen. Spending time with Blake had only one drawback, her attraction to him. Hopefully, by the time this contest was over, her interest would remain under control and wouldn't break her heart.

"What time?"

In for a penny, in for a pound. "How about right after church? You can meet us there and we can head to Lancaster for lunch and ice cream, the old-fashioned way." It was a way for him to experience more of what life was like when you slowed down long enough to appreciate it.

"It's a deal," he said without hesitation. "What time does church get over?"

Zoe shook her head. "That's not what I meant. Meet us before church. It'll be good for you," she teased.

Blake hesitated only a moment. "Sure, why not. It'll make Grandpa happy. Not to mention my dad. He'll probably faint with surprise." He chuckled.

"Good. It's a date. A business date," she corrected.

"But you two aren't dating. Right?" Scott asked, suddenly interested in the grown-ups' conversation.

"No," they both answered in unison.

"Good. I don't want my mom to get hurt the way my dad hurt her when he left. I'm the man of the house now, and I take care of her," her son said, standing tall and moving closer to Zoe. She wrapped an arm around his back and pulled him close.

"Understood, young man." Blake nodded in Scott's direction and smiled.

They got ready to leave the store and Zoe relented, letting Scott pick out three kinds of candy. She wasn't going to be the bad guy in today's adventure. Blake would take those honors when he left Hallbrook.

Chapter Twelve

♥

IT HAD BEEN A moment of insanity, perhaps prompted by Scott's exhilaration and warm smiles, but Zoe's invitation for Blake to join them at church this morning had her spending extra time picking out clothes and fixing her hair. It was cold outside, but still, she'd picked her favorite royal blue sweater dress, adding cream-colored leggings for warmth, and earrings and a necklace to match. Satisfied with her appearance, she headed to the living room.

Some might call it preening; she preferred to think of it as looking her best. She prayed Scott's happy attitude carried over into today since they'd be spending a good portion of it with Blake.

"Scott," she called out. "You about ready to go?"

He came into the living room seconds later. "I'm ready. Wow, you look nice. What's the occasion?" he asked.

Ugh. Even her son had noticed. Maybe she'd gone too far. "Whatever do you mean? It's church, and I like to look nice."

"Not that nice." Scott had the good sense to look embarrassed. "Sorry, I didn't mean anything bad. It's just that you're wearing a dress and we're not going to a wedding or a funeral."

"Stop. That's enough, and I get what you mean. But it is nice to dress up once in a while." She was trying to play it off as no-big-deal, but Scott didn't look convinced.

"This is for Blake, isn't it?" Her son had her pegged and had seen right through to her motives, not that she'd admit it to him.

"No. We're taking him to lunch today as a way to thank Blake for taking us to the city yesterday. It's still just business."

"If you say so," he mumbled, clearly not believing her. At least he wasn't coming right out with a change of attitude with his assumption.

"Let's go." She grabbed her jacket and tossed Scott his. Together, they headed outside and slid into the car. Zoe started the engine, making sure to turn off the fan. The short ride to the church wasn't worth the time or extra chill of a cold blast to get to the warmth.

They arrived at the church, and upon finding a spot available in the parking lot, Zoe grabbed it, grateful they wouldn't have to find one farther away. The cold seemed to have kept some people home or delayed.

After dropping Scott off at the kid's church, she found a seat toward the back for Blake to easily find her. *If he came.* She doubted he'd change his mind and be a no-show, but one never knew.

Five minutes later, he slid in next to her, looking handsome in a blue suit. A perfect complement to her outfit, almost like it was planned.

"Good morning. Just in time I see," Blake said, smiling at her. "Nice outfit. That's the most dressed up I've seen you and I like it." He winked.

"Good morning to you, too. And thank you. I think." She grinned back, not sure how to still her racing heart, his remark making the extra effort she'd put in this morning worth the while. "I was beginning to wonder if you were coming."

"I'm a man of my word. Where's Scott?" he asked.

"Kid's church. He prefers it to the grown-up version."

"Lucky him," Blake countered.

"What's that supposed to mean?" she asked, worried that he hadn't actually been receptive to the invitation and wasn't thrilled to be here.

He shrugged. "Nothing really. It's just that I remember going there every week as a kid and had a lot of fun. Sometimes I wish adult church was more like that."

"So, what I'm hearing is that you're a big kid. You could always dance to the praise team music as they sing." She laughed, poking him in the ribs. The camaraderie between them helped her to relax.

Mrs. O'Malley turned from the row in front of them and smiled, nodding her head in approval.

"Uh-oh. We're in trouble," Zoe whispered under her breath while smiling back at the woman.

"Why? What did we do?" Blake asked.

"We came here together. We sure didn't think this out. It's one thing to go to the city or to Lancaster where no one would see or know us, but here, the whole town is an eye witness to us spending time together without Scott. In church, no less. Tongues will be wagging." She shook her head, knowing exactly what the gossips would be saying.

Blake looked around the room and then back at her. "So, let them. It's not that we didn't try to make our position clear. And in the end, they'll find out they're wrong about us."

"Easy for you to say when you ride off into the sunset." Not to mention the issue it would present with Scott.

Blake leaned closer. "*If* I ride off into the sunset. I may not," he said, keeping his voice low.

The problem with his answer was that if it were true, it would have meant she'd lost the contest, the promotion, and the prize money. Not a happy thought for her. Although him leaving, she realized, would also leave a void. She'd enjoyed having him around this past week, even if they were on opposite sides. If they were on the same team, they'd be terrific together. *Maybe.* It took two, and every chance Blake got, it seemed he was reminding her he wasn't the relationship kind of guy.

But then, why was he in church with her? And why were they spending so much time together? Were they really trying to sway the other person to fall in line with their viewpoint, or was there more to it? For Zoe, she wasn't sure anymore.

The praise team started the first song, and Zoe happily fell silent to listen. They both stood, clapping their hands to the beat, the room lights dimming. Zoe let the last of her worries go, the music lifting her mood and filling her with the spirit of God and love, as she joined in the singing. Blake's deep voice next to her took her by surprise. Even more so when he took her hand and squeezed.

Her heart raced in triple time. Blake's mixed messages were confusing at best and would be heartbreaking if she made the mistake of falling in love with him. Something that very well may have already happened.

What about Scott? Her son's acceptance of Blake would change if he knew the truth of Zoe's affections. It was a fine line to walk, but one she'd try to stay the course.

Soon enough, Blake would go back to the city, and she'd be left with the memories of what little time they shared together. Which was a far sight better than she'd been left with after her high school crush crashed and burned when he started dating Tammy Wright.

The lights came on, and Blake dropped her hand, unwilling to let the whole town see his overt friendly gesture. The pastor came out to preach, and they sat, ready to listen and take notes if needed. The message was on seeing with your eyes wide open, focusing on the future, and not dwelling on the past. The path one chooses is a journey, and each person's journey is different. But the result should be to draw closer to God, letting that dictate your personal choices.

It was a lot to take in and it gave her much to think about. *Later.* At this moment, her journey was to pick up Scott and for the three of them to head to Lancaster.

"That was good, don't you think?" Blake asked as they joined the line to leave.

"Absolutely. Pastor Richard's words are always uplifting. He has a gift for making one think about life and the pursuit of happiness." They turned right and headed down the hall toward the kids' area.

"And what's your take on it?" he asked.

"That happiness comes from love in your heart. And love comes from a faith in Jesus and is a gift from God if one chooses to embrace it." Zoe recounted what she'd learned a few years back. She'd turned to God for understanding after her marriage fell apart and for guidance. The answers had been there all along; it had simply been up to her to find them.

"Interesting. So, without love, you think there's no happiness?" Blake asked.

"How can there be? Look around you; where there's love, there are smiles and joy and light. It's easy to be carried away by the moment and think something is love, but then the happiness is fleeting. With real love, it's lasting." It was an odd conversation to be having with Blake. Her crush on him had been one of those fleeting moments. The problem now, though, was she wasn't sure her feelings toward him fell under the same category.

"Is this about the message or about you trying to sell me on your renovation ideas?" He grinned.

"Maybe both." She shrugged. It was a safe response, but the only one she was willing to give.

"Honest answer. I like that about you."

"At least we have one thing in common—we're both honest to the core." She stopped in front of Scott's room to wait for him to come out.

"Make that two. Don't forget the Maple Nut ice cream," he teased.

"But it's not your favorite," she countered, enjoying the moment.

Blake chuckled. "It might be. I'll never tell."

Scott came out, preventing her from answering. "Hey, there. Did you have a good time?" Zoe asked.

Her son shrugged, looking back and forth between her and Blake. "It was all right, I guess."

Zoe frowned. "Well, that's very non-committal."

Her son's face scrunched up in distaste. "I was having fun until Jenny Lou Miller teased me about my freckles."

"Oh, Scott. Teasing is a way of saying you like someone. At least the non-hurtful kind of teasing," she explained. It would seem her son had his first admirer. He was growing up fast, something she wasn't ready for.

Scott's face flushed bright red.

"Interesting perspective." Blake grinned and winked at her, out of Scott's view. "There's this girl—"

"Stop. I think we can do without a story about your love life." She laughed.

"Grown-ups. You two are weird. Besides, it's not like that. Why do girls think everything is about mushy stuff?" Scott shook his head, the truth not settling well with her son.

"Because we believe in love."

"I don't," her son insisted; his protest over the top for a boy of nine.

Zoe laughed. "You will, trust me. When the time is right, you can't stop it from happening."

Blake held the door for them to pass through. "Your mother's right."

"How would you know? You're not married, and you own a helicopter and work for a big company. And you drive a Porsche. That's my kind of happiness. Johnny's older brother comes home once in a while and he tells us great stories. He's got lots of money too *and* he looks happy."

Zoe shook her head. Her son was naïve to the world and only saw what he wanted to. "You should have been in the adult church this morning. The pastor preached on that very subject. Love is where lasting happiness comes from."

"Blake's happy, aren't you?" Scott looked up at Blake for confirmation.

"But will it last?" Zoe answered for Blake. "When the next car comes out, or the helicopter ride is over, what's left? You lose interest in the car you have, and then you're looking for something else to do to fill your time and make you happy. Those are fleeting joys."

"She has a point, Scott. The exhilaration is only as good as long as the action doesn't stop," Blake joined in the conversation, surprising her with his comment.

"And then you go home—alone. Scott and I have each other, so we go home and the love we share is still there after the excitement of a day like yesterday wears off."

"Another good point, one I've never thought about."

"I'm hungry," Scott announced, clearly bored with the direction the conversation had taken.

"Let's go then. I'll drive since someone here only has a two-seater." Zoe couldn't help but tease him.

Blake frowned. "Another downside of my car."

They made it to her car and got in, the car taking its sweet time to heat up enough for her to flip on the heater. Scott sat in the back, not talking much, except when something they passed by caught his interest.

Thirty minutes later, she parked down the street from one of her favorite places. "We're here," she announced. "Luigi's for lunch."

"I love Luigi's," Scott piped up.

They entered the small five and dime shop and made their way to the back where food was served, passing displays of old-fashioned candy, herbal remedies, and anything else one expected to find in a one-stop-shop. Old-time charm radiated from every inch of the place, the owner having restored the drugstore to its original 1950s appearance. The small counter bar offered guests the full experience as he served lunch and ice cream sodas.

"Wow. Nice place. I don't remember ever hearing about it," Blake said, looking around as they headed down the aisle.

"You wouldn't have. You're a city boy now and this place was renovated about three years ago. I try to come here at least a couple of times a month. I love the hardwood floors, the smell of peppermint and spice, and the occasional sound of the train above our heads blowing its whistle."

They took seats on the red leather-topped stools just as the server placed menus on the black and white checked Formica counter. "Good afternoon, folks. What can I get you to drink?"

"Give us a minute. It's my friend's first time." She nodded toward Blake.

"Sounds good. And welcome to Luigi's," the server said, smiling at him. Zoe couldn't tell if it was from genuine friendliness or more because Blake was a handsome hunk, and the girl was in a flirty mood.

"Thank you." He nodded and turned to Zoe. "What's good here?"

"There are several classic burger specials, and for the kid at heart, there are some crazy choices like a grilled peanut butter and jelly sandwich. Although, that's one I can't honestly say I've tried."

"I have. It's yummy," Scott said, joining in the conversation.

"Oh, and for drinks, you can't go wrong with a malted milkshake or an ice cream soda. The soda is fresh from a fountain. And save room for dessert. They have homemade ice cream."

"Where is this different than what you could get at the candy shop? At least there, more than one employee is always available to take care of things. This could take a while." Blake glanced down the counter, his gaze taking in the scene.

"It's meant to be slow. Time to digest. Relax. And you can hear yourself think." Zoe had hoped he would see reason—maybe even back out of the contest and admit she was right. Except he was acting like it was a lost cause.

Zoe loved the stainless-steel shaker cups served with an iced mug, the soda pop machine that mixed a drink from syrup and carbonated water, and all the vintage signs. The place even had a pay phone in one corner and a vintage jukebox in the other. An old classic song was playing, one that helped put

Zoe in the mood to unwind and enjoy her lunch, even if Blake couldn't understand the impact.

She'd once visited Goolrick's Pharmacy in Virginia, the oldest soda fountain in the U.S, and she'd left feeling bowled over by the trip back in time. That's how she wanted Peterson's to look. Luigi even dressed the part of a soda jerk, not that she'd make the staff go that far. But perhaps some old-time aprons and hats would be a nice touch.

"I want the PB & J and an ice-cold lemonade, Mom," Scott said, spinning around on the barstools. It was something he loved to do ever since Luigi had given him permission to sit-and-spin, telling Zoe it was a kid's favorite.

"Sure thing. Grilled, right?" she asked.

He grabbed the counter and stopped spinning. "Yup. Can I have a nickel to play the pinball machine?"

"I don't see why not." Zoe looked in her wallet to find him some change, handing Scott extra coins. He moved off, on to the next fun thing to do. The machine had seen better days, but the flippers still worked, and the balls still rolled. It was a favorite of her son's. Without tons of kids around, it was just him and the machine and the music and some good ol' country fun.

"A nickel? Sounds cheap. Does the machine even work?" Blake asked, his tone in doubting Thomas mode.

Zoe nodded and laughed. "Of course it does. A nickel is what it used to cost when the place first opened. Not everything is about money."

"Says the assistant manager at Peterson's."

His comment stung, mostly because it was true. "Touché. Speaking of, are you coming in tomorrow? Things will be a little hectic because it's a teacher workday. I couldn't take it off because there's so much to do at the shop."

Blake nodded. "I am, but only because I have a meeting with someone to discuss the renovations at one."

"Be forewarned, it could be noisy. Teacher workday also means lots of kids will come to the shop throughout the day." Zoe shot him a smile. A meeting wouldn't be an easy thing to pull off and they'd more than likely be in the way, but she'd deal with it. She'd promised to give him full access to the place.

"Consider me warned. Scott will enjoy the day there, I'm sure."

"Not really," she said.

Blake's eyebrow's shot up in surprise. "What kid doesn't like hanging out at an ice cream shop all day?"

"The kind who prefers to play outdoors."

"I see. On the other hand, growing up, I would have preferred the shop."

"The old one or the new one, the way you want to set it up?" she asked, if only to make him remember what it was that made him prefer the shop. She wasn't above using his own memories to convince him of what was right.

Blake paused, his forehead wrinkled as he thought about her question. "Honestly, I'm not sure. If I say the old one, you won't let go and will call it a win. On the other hand, the new will be more profitable, and that's why I'm trying to show my grandfather a way to increase profits through streamlined growth. Besides, how the place looked would have had nothing to do with my choice."

"What did?" she asked, curious what would have motivated a young Blake.

"Not doing farm work. Anything was better." He grinned.

She should have known it would be something single-minded. "Okay, so that's not what I'm after. Let me rephrase. Which one has a better feel?"

"Why go country fresh when you can have fifty flavors fast and never get bored?" Blake shot her a grin. Blake wasn't giving an inch, and his comment was a reminder why she'd be a fool to fall for him.

"Because it's unfulfilling to change flavors every day and not know which one you prefer."

"Are we still talking about renovations?"

"Only if you are." She'd drifted way off-topic, his comment about country fresh as boring had been a direct hit against her. Call it another warning, but this time she was standing her ground. The guy needed to grow up, and life included relationships. At some point, running from them would only leave a person empty.

Something she needed to take her own advice for. Maybe it was time to put herself back out there and stop hiding behind Scott. And if not Blake because he was a stubborn mule, then someone else. Someone who had the capacity to love whole-heartedly.

Chapter Thirteen

♥

Hanging up the phone after talking to Tammy Wright, Blake's schedule for the day was suddenly cleared. Truthfully, he didn't mind putting off what he considered an unavoidable meeting. And it was the perfect opportunity to go ice fishing. The excitement of spending the day on the ice grew with each passing minute as he located all his gear and loaded the cargo area of the four-wheeler.

Backing up the UTV to the fishing shanty, he hooked it to the hitch. Blake took a deep breath, the fresh but cold country air and snow, causing him to pull his jacket closed and zip it all the way up. It was almost Easter, and soon, the cold days would be a thing of the past as spring moved closer to summer. The icy cold breezes that sometimes whipped up were the only thing he didn't enjoy on an outing such as this, but he'd be inside the shanty, and he'd packed plenty of hand warmers.

Suddenly, an image of Zoe standing over a fire, smiling up at him, hit Blake hard in the chest. Long flowing brown hair dancing as she moved. Why was he thinking of her when he should be thinking about the fish he was going to haul in? He needed to call and let her know he wouldn't be in today. A courtesy call.

Yeah, right. The pleasure of talking to her was an added bonus he didn't mind one bit and offered a greater incentive than mere courtesy. Blake called the creamery, preferring not to use Zoe's direct number even though she'd given it to him. It was too personal and friendly, and this was business.

"Good morning, Peterson's Ice Creamery. How may I help you?" Lindsey answered the phone. He was finally getting to know faces and names at the shop which was a step in the right direction.

"Good morning, Lindsey. This is Blake Peterson. Is Zoe around by any chance?"

"She sure is. Hold on, and I'll get her."

Blake waited several minutes before he heard the phone being picked up.

"Hey there. Sorry it took so long to answer. Scott is having a difficult time settling down this morning, and I was cleaning up some spilled cocoa. I've got my hands full today, that's for sure." She spoke in a rush, her frustration coming through the line loud and clear.

"That doesn't sound good, but don't worry about it. I've got plenty of time. I only called to tell you my meeting was canceled, and I won't be in today." The fish were calling his name and he was anxious to get out on the ice. He was more than ready to take a day off of work.

"Bummer, I could have used your help. I would have stuck with the jobs of babysitter and server extraordinaire." Her tinkling laughter was something a man could get used to.

"I'm not sure I deserve either role." He chuckled. "But I'm passable as a server, so I might be passable as a sitter." The words rolled out of his mouth without much thought, but it was too late to call them back. It was nothing short of an offer to watch Scott at the creamery, although the reality wasn't even close.

"Be careful what you say, or you'll find yourself eating ice cream and drinking cocoa with a kid who's on hyperdrive all day. Unless, of course, that is a real offer?" she asked, hope in her voice.

Blake wavered, searching for a way to backstroke the offer without sounding cowardly. "Or I could pick him up and take him with me. I'm going ice fishing." It was the best he could think of on short notice, although he was sure he'd just made the biggest mistake of his life. What did he know about entertaining a kid, especially one who was still on the fence whether he even liked him?

"Ice fishing? You're kidding, right?" she asked.

"Yes, ice fishing. Fishing is where I do my best creative thinking." It was true; he'd just never tried it with a kid in tow.

"Wow. I would have expected you prefer your thinking in a shark tank or something," Zoe teased.

As much as he liked fishing, sharks were not on his agenda—in or out of a tank. Talk about stressful. "Very funny."

"Ummm, you wouldn't happen to be serious about taking Scott though, are you?" she asked hesitantly.

Blake decided to go all in. Anything to make Zoe happy or ease the pressure she was under. He was positive she was overworked and underpaid already. "Sure, why not? You said he likes being outdoors. Being in the shanty in the cold and dropping a line through the ice definitely still counts as being outside last time I checked."

"I don't know. Are you sure it's safe this time of year?" Zoe was having second thoughts, as any mom would in this situation.

"It's a small well-stocked pond at the back of our property. The ice is plenty thick enough for ice fishing safely. Trust me. I've fished this pond since I was a kid." He'd come a full circle from trying to find a way out of his offer to convincing Zoe it would be good for Scott, all in the space of thirty seconds. Blake rolled his eyes and shook his head, amazed at the change.

"Okay, then. There's also the issue of how he feels about you—or should I say you and me together. Ummm, you know what I mean. We know we're not together, but Scott's worried we are, and this might push him over the edge." Zoe stumbled over the words, clearly uncomfortable talking about the two of them as a couple. No more so than he was; something else they had in common.

"Just ask him, will you? It'll help you both out. Besides, how hard can it be? Just two guys out fishing. Tell him Hank will be there—that should sway his decision."

"Fine, I'll ask. Hang on."

Blake was torn whether he wanted Scott to say yes or no. He'd been sure he could do it while talking with Zoe, but the truth was, he was anything but confident. It was the dual persona he'd carried with him since high school. Show the world one thing, but keep any weakness hidden from plain sight—a motto that had served him well.

"I'm back. Looks like you got yourself a fishing partner. He tried to act all cool about it, but he's never been fishing, ice fishing or otherwise. Larry never took the time, and I don't know the first thing about it."

"Larry's loss, my gain. And it sounds like I need to take you fishing as well. No one should reach adulthood without having gone fishing a time or two, especially if you live in the country. Most of the time it's a lesson in patience, but there is the big payout of a thrill when you do catch a fish." There were plenty of times he never caught anything, but when the fish hit, all the previous skunks disappeared, and it was just him and the fish in a battle of wills.

"I'll have to trust you on that." She hadn't said anything about his offer to take her some time, and he decided to let it drop. First, he had to get through a day with Scott. "I'll swing by and pick him up at the creamery. Tell him to be ready by the front door. I'll be in the truck."

"Sounds good. And Blake, thank you. It really is a sweet offer and a much appreciated one," Zoe said, her voice dropping slightly lower, but he managed to piece it together.

"Don't worry about it. It'll be fine. This way, you can concentrate on your nostalgia design renovations, and come Easter, you won't be able to blame your loss on not being able to concentrate." Blake grinned, knowing his comment would rub her the wrong way. He wasn't a big teaser, but around Zoe, it came easy.

"Laugh now, but you're the one who'll be crying when this is over. You think you're in for a thinking day—well, think again. But don't say I didn't warn you." Zoe was quick with a comeback, her warning taking him by surprise. Scott was just a kid, one out of diapers and who didn't need help eating or going to the bathroom. He was almost grown-up in caring for himself. How much trouble could a nine-year-old be? It was going to be a good day, regardless of what Zoe thought.

"You can't scare me. It'll be fine, just you wait and see. Be there in fifteen minutes."

Zoe's laughter rang out before the line disconnected.

Blake walked back to the house to get the truck and Hank, grabbing the dog's paw socks off the counter since they would be out on the ice.

"Hank, here boy." The dog came barreling toward him. "Change of plans, you lucky devil. You're coming fishing. I figure you can keep up with Scott and keep him entertained if he gets bored." Blake pulled open the door to let his furry friend pass through first.

Woof. Woof.

Chapter Fourteen

♥

FORTY-FIVE MINUTES LATER, BLAKE had the extra fishing gear needed for Scott loaded. It had been a happy reunion between the boy and Hank, the dog going into a full-body-wiggle mode when he spotted his new friend. With everyone ready to roll, Blake put the UTV in gear and followed the trail. It didn't take long to get to the pond on the back forty. "This is it," Blake said, as he came to a stop before they crossed onto the ice.

"Where are all the people? Why isn't anyone else fishing?" Scott looked at him, a questioning expression revealing his doubts this was a legitimate fishing trip.

Blake let out a deep breath, the moisture creating a patch of fog. "It's a private pond. A private, stocked pond," he clarified. "Which, to you and me, means plenty of fish. The trick is catching them." He laughed, trying to ease the tension between them, and find a way to connect. Otherwise, it would be a long afternoon.

"But it's covered in ice. How do we get the bait to the fish?" he asked, pointing at the pond.

"That's why they call this ice fishing. I'm going to pull the shanty out about fifty yards and set it down. Once we're inside, I'll set us with a source of heat and then we can auger a couple of openings through the ice. You drop a line through the hole—and then wait."

"So, it's not real fishing. Like I don't cast or anything special." Scott's downcast expression tugged at Blake's heart. The kid didn't understand yet, but hopefully, before long, he'd change his tune.

"It's fishing, and quite challenging. Some of the toughest fishing you'll ever do. You have to be creative to get the fish to bite as they don't typically eat much in the winter months. Things like moving your line around just right, so they decide to take your free food offering." Blake tried to explain it in a way Scott would understand and hopefully catch interest. With any luck, the kid would catch a fish or two. Blake never forgot his first fish. Or his best fishing day. Or any number of other memorable fishing trips that occurred over the years.

"What if we fall through the ice?" Scott asked, still full of questions

"It's safe this time of year. Trust me on this. I used to fish here every winter from the time I was about five until I left home. Years of experience and understanding the weather conditions leading up to now." His father was the one who taught Blake to answer questions to the extreme, hoping to put an end to them. Time would tell if the method worked with Scott. Although, back then, once Blake discovered it meant his dad wanted him to be quiet, he quit asking questions. Not the case now.

"Okay, if you're sure," the kid said hesitantly, although he didn't look convinced.

Blake put the UTV in gear and moved forward, this time going extremely slow, using caution as his guide. He wanted to keep all the supplies balanced as they moved down the gently sloped bank and crept out onto the ice, not wanting to dump anything off the back. He listened intently for creaks and groans that would mean the ice was shifting, and early indicator of a soft spot. Easter was typically the cut off around here, and the closer you got to it, the more you paid attention.

Nothing out of the ordinary happened, and he trusted his instincts, making his way to one of his favorite spots. Hank had a mind of his own, and jumped down. He started running around in circles, occasionally stopping to sniff the air.

Scott tentatively stepped down off the UTV. The kid's confidence growing with each step, until soon, he was following Hank around, leaving Blake to setup. He lowered the ramps and slid the shanty down off the trailer to the ice.

Blake transferred the poles, the bait, and the food he'd packed into the shanty. Going back for his portable fire Sterno and the auger, he glanced over at the pair to make sure they were doing okay. "Hey, Scott, come watch this," he called out.

Scott ran in his direction, Hank hot on his heels. Blake pushed the door open with his foot. "Go on in; I'm right behind you."

Inside, Scott looked back at him. "Wow. This is cool. *Ummm*, won't the fire melt the ice?" he asked as Blake tried to light the Sterno heater.

"This kind of fire won't. It's not actually touching the ice the way it's set up. It's mainly used for a little extra warmth in the shanty. We've got hand warmers for inside your gloves. Of course, it's good to keep the coffee hot, too." Blake chuckled.

"I can't drink coffee. Mom says I'm too young," Scott said, a look of disappointment on his face.

"*Hmmm.* I hadn't thought of that. Well, maybe this one time, we can break the rules. It helps to keep you warm, and I'm sure she'd be okay with that."

Scott grinned. "Okay. Rule-breaking with permission. I don't get that often."

Blake started to second-guess his offer. What if Zoe wasn't happy with his decision? A call might be in order. Scott's expression was the deciding factor. The kid was happy, and Blake wasn't going to risk changing his mood. He'd deal with Zoe later.

Hank moved to the corner where Blake had laid out his blanket. The dog curled up but kept watch over everything they did.

"So, this here is a power auger. It takes a lot of strength to hold it in place, but I wanted you to watch how it works. The first thing is for you to decide where you want to fish," Blake explained.

"I don't know. It's not like this shanty is very big. How about right here? Close to the fire." Scott pointed to a spot about a foot and a half away from the Sterno.

"Good choice, son."

Scott shot him a look, one that spoke volumes, but the kid kept silent. The word had slipped out, Blake meaning it more like a young man name. *Friendly*. In hindsight, it probably carried a far deeper connotation to a nine-year-old. One who's own father wasn't in the picture.

Blake powered on the auger, the loud engine echoing through the shanty.

Scott covered his ears and watched.

Holding on tight, Blake pressed down, letting the sharp blades catch on the surface and begin to dig. Inch by inch, the auger churned up ice crystals, piling them all around the new hole. It took about ten minutes to break through the final sheet of ice and the water was exposed. He shut the machine off.

"*Ummm...*That's pretty cool. Can I try?" Scott asked.

"I'm not sure that's a good idea." Coffee was one thing, and an auger, well, that was different.

"Figures. I never get to do anything grown-up. I'm responsible and get good grades in school," Scott said, his voice taking on a petulant tone.

"I like to hear that. I'm sure your mom is right proud of you." Blake wanted to say yes to the kid. He wanted Scott to like him. And he wanted the day to go well. But the machine was dangerous. Common sense overruled scoring likeable points. "I tell you what. I'll get it started, and then why don't we work together on holding it steady as it digs?" By way of compromise, it was as good an offer he could give.

"You mean it?" Scott's eyes were wide as saucers, his happy smile back in place. Blake's father hadn't let him use the auger with or without him until he was sixteen. Said it was a man's job. But Scott was a little man in a hurry to grow up. With Blake helping, it would be fine, and Scott didn't seem to mind the backup muscle. He just wanted more freedom and to explore new things. No harm in that, at least not to Blake's way of thinking.

It took a little longer, but when the auger broke through to the water, Scott looked up at him, his eyes shining bright. "Can I have this hole since I dug it?"

"Absolutely."

Blake took the auger back to the UTV, returning with the chairs. He set them up before grabbing the pole he'd brought for Scott. Putting on the minnow, he turned to the kid. "For this reel, simply flip the bar, and let your minnow drop down into the hole. The pond is about twenty feet deep and you can try to fish at any level, although they tend to hang at the bottom where it's the warmest. When you have it where you want it, flip the bale over to lock it in place. Then move your pole around and see if you have any luck attracting the fish." Blake showed him once, dropping a line through the hole to emphasize what needed to happen. Telling and showing had always worked well for him as a kid.

"That's it? Seems easy enough." Scott shrugged, taking the pole from him. Following instructions, the kid dropped the line into the water, stopping it about ten feet down. "Now what?" he asked.

Blake chuckled. "We wait." This was the hard part for any kid—especially first timers.

"That's it? Sounds boring," he mumbled.

"Yes, that's it. Fishing is about patience. When you catch a fish, it makes the wait all worthwhile. Trust me. There's no greater feeling than the success of landing a fish, more so if it's a great catch. Half the fun is reeling in to find out what's on the line. It's like digging to the bottom of a Cracker Jack box for the surprise." Blake laughed.

"I love Cracker Jacks. Sometimes I get cool tattoos, but sometimes the prizes are lame. Like little books, or worse—a tiny plastic doll." Scott scrunched up his face.

Blake shook his head and grinned. The kid was turning out to be a talker. Who knew?

Hank got up, tugging his blanket closer to the boy before laying back down. Scott reached down to pet him, letting his hand absently stroke the dog. There was a strong bond forming between the two. Hank hadn't bonded this tightly with anyone else since he'd rescued the dog years ago.

An hour passed, the conversation non-stop. Along with a few huffs and puffs in between checking his line—just in case, Scott was quickly growing bored. Not a single catch between them. And not a single minute for Blake to relax and think.

Scott didn't need taking care of like a toddler, but Blake was quickly coming to the realization kids needed attention, something far more time consuming than a diaper change.

"Where are the fish? This is boring." Scott kicked his feet back and forth, swinging them in the air.

"Be patient. Some days, I don't catch a thing. It's all about the chance of catching something."

Scott let out a deep breath. "I'm cold."

"Then warm up by standing closer to the fire. You can put your back to the warmth and dangle your fishing line in the water. Then you can still feel it if something bites on your hook."

The peace lasted for all of five minutes before Scott turned back to face him. "I'm hungry."

"There's a couple of sandwiches in the basket and some hot tomato soup in the thermos. Just be careful you don't spill it and burn yourself." Blake was trying to cover all the bases, the parenting thing not natural for him.

"I can't get the stupid lid off," Scott mumbled.

Blake got up to help him, pouring some into the lid that served as a cup.

"Thanks." Zoe had taught the kid good manners. Patience, however, was in short supply. Or maybe this was all kids doing anything. Perhaps that was what Zoe was alluding to in her comment about no thinking time. The more he thought about it, he was sure he was right. *It was going to be a long afternoon.*

Scott picked up his fishing pole and bounced it around. "*Ummm*, I think a fish bit my minnow. It felt weird," he said, excitement in his voice.

"Does it feel like something is on there? It would be pulling away and wouldn't be overly happy with a hook in its mouth." Thinking you felt a bite was a long way from actually having one. Countless times he remembered his father admonishing him for his lack of patience, always wanting to check the line.

"No. But what if the fish took my minnow? Maybe I should check," he asked, starting to reel in his line a few turns. There'd be no end to it if Blake didn't let him check.

"Sure, why not," Blake said, more than happy to let the kid entertain himself.

Scott started to reel in his line a little faster. "Whoa, I got something," he exclaimed, his eyes growing wide, a huge smile on his face. "I got one. I got one. What do I do?"

Sure enough, the pole was bobbing, pulling down toward the hole in the ice as the fish tried to swim away. "Set the hook by giving it a sharp jerk back once. Just to make sure he's hooked good."

The kid did as he was told and then looked at Blake. "Now what?"

"Now it's time to find out what you got. And I'm guessing it won't be a plastic doll." Blake grinned. "Keep reeling. Slow and steady. That's it. You're doing great." Blake stood next to him, ready to help with a net if needed. The last thing he wanted was for the kid's first fish to get away.

The fish splashed at the surface, and Blake reached down to pull the line and fish out through the hole. He held up a young second-year bass, about eight inches long.

"What is it?" Scott asked, his expression one of pure joy.

"This is called a large-mouth bass. See how big his mouth opens when I lip him with my thumb to hold him in place as I remove the hook?" Blake reached into the fish's mouth and unhooked him, the fish barely on.

"Can I touch him?" Scott asked.

Blake smiled, remembering the joy of his own first fish. It was a huge moment in a kid's life. "Of course, he's your fish. Do you want to hold him, and I'll take a picture for your mom?"

"Sure," Scott beamed, reaching out to take the bass and hold him the way Blake had done.

Hank had moved next to Scott, checking out the fish. He sniffed the air and then backed away, causing Scott to laugh. "Don't be afraid, boy. It's just a little ol' fish." The kid was fearless and held on as Blake grabbed his phone out of his back pocket. He took a couple of quick pictures just in case Scott lost his hold and the fish disappeared back in the hole. "One last picture. Extend your arm out and hold the fish at chin level."

"What does that do?" Scott asked. "Seems weird if you ask me."

Blake grinned. "It makes the fish look bigger in the picture." It was an old trick his grandfather had taught him.

"Cool. What do we do with him now? Are we going to cook him and eat him for dinner?"

Blake shook his head. "We're going to let him go. It's called catch and release," he explained, knowing what came next.

"What? I just caught him and now I have to put him back down in the hole and let him go? That doesn't make any sense."

"It's fishing for sport. It lets this little guy grow up, and the next time you catch him he'll be bigger. Just like you keep getting bigger."

Scott's excitement faded, his smile slipping.

"What's wrong?" Blake asked as Scott bent over to put the fish in the hole.

"Nothing," the kid mumbled. "Bye-bye, Mr. Fishy."

"Talk to me, Scott. I can't explain things if you don't ask." Blake knew something was wrong and he was determined to understand and help if he could.

"Well, it's just the fish will grow up, but then I won't get to catch him again." Scott looked away, rubbing Hank's fur down the side of his face.

He didn't understand what Scott meant. "Why do you think you can't catch him again?"

Scott looked up, his expression tense—as though trying to be a tough guy. "I reckon I won't get to fish with you again seeing as you live in the city." The words came out low and soft, with little to no emotion.

It dawned on Blake what he was getting at. "I'll be around, and when I am, I'll bring you fishing."

"You mean it? Really and truly?" Scott's smile was back in place.

"I mean it." Blake wasn't sure what he was promising, but it sounded good to Scott and, he realized, to himself.

The rest of the morning and afternoon wasn't a story he'd forget soon. Scott's non-stop chatter accompanied him catching six more fish, while Blake, on the other hand, got skunked.

In both fish and thinking time.

But it was all good. Scott was who mattered, and a boy's first fishing trip was something he'd never forget. Especially with a seven to zero catch count.

It was a memory Blake wouldn't soon forget either.

Chapter Fifteen

♥

ZOE HAD LONG SINCE left the creamery and was beginning to wonder if she should call Blake to check on them. As if reading her mind, her phone rang, Blake's name flashing across the screen.

"Hey, there. I was just thinking of calling you. Good timing."

"Does that mean you were missing us?" Blake asked.

"Maybe just a little. I got home over an hour ago and have been enjoying the peace and quiet." It was a rare opportunity and one she'd been thoroughly excited about...at least for the first thirty minutes. But after folding the laundry and unloading the dishwasher and a quick vacuum and dusting, she'd sat down in her favorite chair intent on reading. Instead, her mind wandered, only reading three pages over the course of the next thirty minutes, the quiet of the house almost deafening. Either that or she was plumb anxious for the guys to return.

"Sorry to have to change that, but we're on our way back to your place. We reached our maximum of cold exposure." He chuckled.

The image of them shaking and shivering while she was warm and toasty prompted her to return Blake's kindness. "Tell you what, I'll fix you some hot chocolate to help heat you up. And as a way to say thank you for watching Scott and keep him from what would have been utter boredom at the shop, how about I fix you dinner?"

"Now that's an invitation I can't resist," Blake answered, his voice taking on an odd tone. She was pleased the house was clean enough for company considering the impromptu offer. As to the odd tone in his voice, it was better to be safe.

"It's just a thank-you dinner. Don't read anything else into it," she clarified.

"I'm not, trust me. It's the people in town that might think otherwise. But I'm a big boy and can handle the gossip. Can you?" he asked.

"Most definitely. It's almost impossible to avoid the inevitable, so why fight it? It's just like you said, it doesn't change the ending." So why did the very thought of him leaving Hallbrook leave her with a sense of unrest? Falling for Blake would be a huge mistake, and it was one she would fight, if at all possible. Zoe didn't relish nursing another heartache.

"See you in a few. Oh, and by any chance, can you make mine coffee? I grew out of hot chocolate a long time ago."

"Putting the pot on now." They hung up, and Zoe went to work, first by putting some milk on to warm and then prepping a pot of coffee. Her next stop was to figure out what to serve for dinner since none of this had been planned.

She scanned the pantry, her gaze landing on the box of veggie pasta. Spaghetti would be perfect and was one of Scott's favorites. Judging by the amount of time the two had spent together today, Zoe was sure Scott and Blake had bonded over the whole fishing thing. Whether that was good or bad remained to be seen.

She pulled her veggie spaghetti sauce from the freezer and dumped it in a pan, turning the burner on low. It would take a while to thaw, but then she'd add some fresh spices to kick it up a notch. The containers of pre-made sauce came in handy for ready to go meals in a pinch.

Loud chatter coming from the living room announced the guys arrival. She headed for the noise, laughing as they shrugged out of their coats and boots, over-exaggerating how cold they were.

"How did it go today?" Zoe asked, alerting them to her presence.

"It was amazing. You'll never believe it, but I caught seven fish. Blake's promised to take me again and I can't wait to tell all my friends." Scott's eyes were lit with excitement, confirming the two were now getting along.

"Wow. That's exciting. Let me get Blake's coffee and your cocoa first, and then I'll join you by the fire, and you can tell me all about it."

"Scott did great. Are you sure you don't mind Hank coming in?" Blake asked, leaning down to pet the dog.

"Not at all. I love his paw booties and sweater." Zoe grinned. It didn't matter about her clean floors, as family and friends were far more important.

"Thanks. They were a gift from a lady friend, but after we parted ways, I kept them for Hank. I figured they would come in handy for times such as this. I'll throw a couple of extra logs on the fire. Hurry back; we're freezing. A hot beverage is just what we need to warm up our insides. Right, buddy?" he asked, turning to Scott.

"Right." Scott nodded, trudging over to the fireplace and plopping down on the sofa. He grabbed the blanket and wrapped it around him tightly.

Zoe figured there'd been some bonding, but buddies? That was nothing short of a miracle. As to the lady friend, she didn't want to think about the revolving door of his personal life. She headed back to the kitchen and pulled down a tray, placing all the cups on it. She poured the coffee for Blake and added the cocoa and milk to hers and Scott's cups. After stirring them, she added miniature marshmallows to top them off.

Moving back to the living room, she found Blake warming up in front of the fire.

"Here, let me help," he said, reaching for the tray. His gaze connected with hers, and they both paused for the barest hint of a second.

Zoe smiled. "Just take your coffee; I'm fine. Thanks."

Grabbing his cup, Blake paused, glancing at the other cups and then back up at her. "Those look good."

"My mom's recipe is killer. You should have stuck with hot chocolate. Coffee is gross," Scott said, taking the cup Zoe handed him.

"I'll have to remember that next time." Blake winked at her.

"How would you know coffee is gross? I don't remember ever letting you taste it."

Blake and Scott exchanged looks. "I let him have some today. Sorry. We didn't have cocoa and he needed something to help keep him warm. I figured you would forgive me for breaking the rule given the circumstances."

"It's fine. Especially if your coffee was so awful, he's not interested now." Zoe shook her head and laughed. She settled on the sofa next to her son, turning sideways to face him. "So, tell me about the fish you caught. It sounds like you had an exciting day."

"One of them was this big," Scott said, holding his hands about a foot apart. "That was a large-mouth bass, right, Blake?"

"Good memory, buddy." There it was again. *Buddy*. And the two of them were talking like best friends.

"I'm impressed. Although I must admit, I don't even know what that is." Taking a sip of her chocolate, she looked up at Blake. "How many did you catch?"

Blake rolled his eyes and shook his head.

Scott burst out laughing. "He didn't catch any. Just me. Said it wasn't his lucky day, but it sure was mine. I think I jiggled better than he did."

"Jiggled?" she asked, fighting back a laugh, wondering what the heck her son was talking about. Poor Blake. Skunked by a first timer. She'd have to give him an extra helping of dessert for his efforts.

"It's where you move the fishing rod around so the minnow dances in the water and attracts bigger fish to eat him," Scott said with authority, letting his newfound knowledge shine through.

"I see. I still can't believe you caught seven and Blake caught none. That's incredible."

"Don't rub it in," Blake said, a slight hint of a smile giving away merriment at the situation. "Scott's doing a good job of that on his own."

"And Blake promised to take me again. That's okay, right, Mom?" he asked, turning his big blue eyes up to her for permission.

"Of course, honey. So, does that mean you're sticking around after the contest, Blake?" she asked, both out of curiosity and to prepare her son for the disappointment if the next fishing trip never happened. Or, if necessary, she'd take him herself. Then Scott could teach her, and they'd make another special memory of it if she was inept at it as she expected to be. Patience was never a virtue she could claim.

"Depends on what happens, but even if I leave, I'll come back and take him fishing. He caught on fast, and we had loads of fun. Kid can talk a mile a minute, but he's highly entertaining. At least, he was after the first fish. Before that, his patience levels were riding on low."

Like mother, like son. "Sounds like an all-American boy." She chuckled. "Thanks in advance for offering to take him again."

"You're welcome. There wasn't much thinking time, just like you warned me. You've been at this parenting thing a long time, but today was my first day as a role model. Wipes you out—mentally and physically." Blake set his empty cup on the tray and tossed another log on the fire, stirring up the embers until it burned brightly.

"Told you." Zoe couldn't resist capitalizing on the fact she'd been right.

Blake nodded. "Yes, you did. Are you always right about everything?" he asked, one eyebrow raised as he did his best to look pensive.

"Yes. And that includes the contest." Her grin widened, unable to stop teasing him. It wasn't often she had time for friendly chatter in the comfort of her own home, her time spent at the creamery and taking care of Scott and the house. But this...was fun. And something she vowed to do more often. Make time for others in her life outside of church.

"You may have finally met your match," Blake answered, exuding a confidence Zoe couldn't muster.

"I look forward to it. Let me stir the spaghetti sauce and get the noodles started. I'll be right back." She'd learned to put on a good game face for Scott's sake after Larry left. It was a skill that came in handy on occasion.

"I love spaghetti. My mom makes the best homemade sauce ever."

"Seems like Scott is your biggest fan," Blake said, grinning.

"Of course he is." Zoe laughed as she stood. "But I agree, it's good stuff. I only use fresh vegetables. Tomatoes. Zucchini. Yellow squash. Onion. Mushrooms. The first three, I grow in the back yard."

"Wow, so we can add gardener to your extensive list of many talents," Blake said, his smile warming her heart.

"I try. Even the squirrels think my tomatoes are the best. They'd sample a bite from every one of them if I didn't get the tomato off the vine early enough. It's like they know when they're perfectly ripe for the picking."

Blake shook his head. "Tomato-eating squirrels? That's not one I've heard before."

"No one believes me at school either when I tell them," Scott chimed in. "But they'll have to believe me about the fish. Show Mom the pictures you took."

Blake pulled out his phone and tapped a few keys before handing it to her.

Zoe scrolled through the pictures, all roughly twenty plus of them. "These are great. Make sure to send them to me so I can print a couple out to frame." She especially loved the selfie Blake had taken of the two of them grinning like little boys as Scott held up a fish.

"I'll take care of that right now," he said, taking the phone from her outstretched hand.

"Thanks. I really need to go check on the sauce and start the noodles if you two hungry guys plan to eat tonight." Zoe walked out of the room, the two of them immediately delving into another fishing conversation.

Two hours later, they were settled back on the sofa to relax. With dinner and dessert over and everyone chipping in with the dishes, the evening had gone quite well. Zoe was just about to offer they play a game when Scott suddenly yawned.

Her son was clearly worn out. "Ready to head to bed, little man?"

Scott frowned. "Bed. I'm too old to go to bed this early," he said, shaking his head as he covered another yawn.

"That maybe, but you've had a big day. Time to dream of the fish and the next one you'll catch," Zoe said, ruffling his hair.

"I like the sound of that. It'll be this big," Scott said, his arms spread wide.

"We better have a bigger hole for a whopper that size." Blake chuckled. "Goodnight, and thanks for spending the day with me, buddy—even if you did skunk me."

"It was good. Real good. Thanks, Blake. I'll remember this day forever," Scott said with enthusiasm.

"Because it was your first fishing trip, and you caught a lot of fish?" Zoe asked, letting her son bask in the glory a moment longer.

"Well, that, but also because it was seven to zero. My luckiest day ever." Scott grinned, ducking away as Blake reached for him.

"Careful, buddy, or next time it'll be me who catches all the fish," Blake said, the laughter in his voice refreshing as the two of them teased back and forth.

"Nah. I know how to jiggle good." Scott flashed him a broad smile before he raced down the hall to his room.

"Good kid," Blake said, nodding. "I should probably head out as well. I need to feed Hank, and I doubt you have any dog food handy." He stood and stretched. Hank looked up from where he lay by the fire, interested in Blake's actions but not enough to make an effort to get up.

"That I don't." She rose and walked beside him toward the front door.

Blake pulled on his coat and boots, Hank finally acknowledging it was time to move and face the fact they were going back outside.

"Thanks for taking Scott out today. You've made a huge impression. I think it's safe to say he's over any negative feelings toward you."

"We made a good team." Blake leaned forward, the anticipation of what was to come racing down her body just as his lips descended on hers. "Thank you," he said, pulling back far too quickly for her liking. "And good night." He pulled open the door and stepped out onto the porch, the cold air chilling her.

"Good night," she said, wrapping her arms around herself to ward off the chill. Hank raced ahead of Blake, and when they reached the truck, Zoe waved and closed the door.

Scott would be dreaming of fish tonight, whereas Zoe was sure her dreams would be centered more on Blake. It was a fool's mission, but for as long as he was in town, she wanted to bask in his friendship and let Scott enjoy having a male role model around. She hadn't seen Scott this excited since Christmas morning. Come to think of it, *she* hadn't felt this alive since Christmas morning either. Christmas magic always had a way of making things wonderful. And Blake was quickly moving into the same category.

Something that would end when the contest was over. One of them had to lose.

Chapter Sixteen

♥

LIFE WAS BACK TO normal for Zoe for the past two days, or almost anyway. Around Blake, normal had changed. Yesterday, the two of them talked and joked as they worked together, earning several odd looks from the staff. But acting like they *weren't* friends would have been wrong, considering all that Blake had done for Scott on Monday.

She glanced at her watch. Not that she was keeping up with him or anything, but he'd mentioned he would be at the shop by noon. It was five minutes till then, and punctuality was his thing.

Zoe finished mixing a batch of Pecan Praline ice cream and added it to the back freezer to allow it time to set up. She picked up all the dishes that needed cleaning and carried them to the sink. Another quick glance at her watch and the front door confirmed Blake was late. Rinsing the bowl with warm water, she placed it on a dry towel and went to work on the utensils.

"You look like little Miss Suzy Homemaker in that apron and doing dishes," Blake said, coming up on her left side and startling her as the water hit the ladle and sprayed, soaking her shirt and apron, some of it hitting Blake in the face. "Well, now, that's what I call a warm welcome."

Zoe tried to calm her racing heart. Lost deep in thought, his sudden presence had thrown her for a loop. "I'm sorry. You scared me."

"That much is obvious." He grinned, using his shirt sleeve to wipe the water off his face. Blake grabbed a towel off the counter and reached out to help her dry off from the soaking.

Zoe grabbed his hand before he reached his target, her face immediately flushing hotter than the warm water. "Thanks. I think I'll take care of the front of my shirt myself. You can wipe the counter, wise guy."

Blake chuckled. "Good point."

Zoe removed the apron and then brushed her sleeves where the water had splashed. "Where did you come from anyway? I've been watching for you."

"It's nice to know you care. I came in the front door, just like everyone else normally does," Blake said, folding the towel and putting it next to the sink. It was the grin he couldn't wipe off his face that kept her off-kilter.

"Don't get any ideas, wise guy. It's not like you to be late so I was worried something was wrong. That's all. You must have come in right when I went to the back freezer and I missed your arrival."

"I liked thinking you cared better." He winked. "Sorry about your shirt. Do you have a change in your office?"

Zoe shook her head. "No, but it'll dry quick enough. Don't worry. So, what's on your agenda today?" She pulled a new apron off the wall and tied it around her back, trying to act nonchalant.

"I'm trying to finalize a few things, and I still needed some specific measurements for counter and table placement—that sort of thing. How about you? Things wrapping up with your designs?"

"Same. Our final team meeting is tonight. I can't believe we're down to today and tomorrow before we turn in our renovation drawings." Zoe had worked on the proposal long after Blake left last night. She'd hoped it would take her mind off the distraction he presented, but her efforts only worked while she was researching and drawing the new image. The minute she turned off the computer and climbed into bed, her thoughts had gone back to Blake. It had been nice of him to spend the afternoon with Scott. More than nice. Scott had gained a new best friend, and as for her, she feared she'd gained a new heart filled with love and ripe for the heartache sure to follow.

"It's gone by fast because I've been in good company." Blake winked. It was exactly those kinds of comments that set her heart to racing.

Lindsey walked by, shooting Zoe an odd look. "Fraternizing with the enemy, Zoe?" She shook her head and walked to the register to wait on a customer.

"Why does everyone think we can't be friends?" Zoe asked, preferring to dwell on the girl's comment rather than Blake's.

"I think it's more of a case of shouldn't than can't. We're on opposite sides of this contest, and everyone wants to win. I reckon they want to make sure everything is fair and square between us. There's a lot of money riding on this," Blake offered.

Zoe nodded, knowing he was right. "Tell me about it." But what about the fact they were people, and people had feelings. In her case, the feelings ran deeper than she would have thought possible. It made no sense to fall for a guy who was emotionally unavailable, but at least he'd never know.

"Ignore them. We both know the truth. We're simply two grown-ups who like each other and are competing against one another. Can't people do that and get along?" It was as though he'd read her mind.

"Absolutely. And then there's Scott—your new buddy. Luckily, they don't know about that part, or I'd never hear the end of it." She lowered her voice as she spoke, not wanting anyone else to hear this part of the conversation. "Speaking of never hearing the end of it, Scott has been asking non-stop when the two of you are going fishing again. I keep telling him the contest is important to both of us and you're busy finalizing your submission. It's buying you some time, but it won't work forever. To a child, your promise meant soon. Children don't think long term. It's like days waiting for something good to happen is like an eternity." He wasn't used to children, and it made sense to clue him into Scott's way of thinking.

"I'll take him again soon, I promise."

"I will pass that along. Maybe it will buy me some time off from his constant interest in the subject." Zoe laughed. "Let me load the dishwasher, and I'll help you with those measurements." It was far better to work than to stand around fraternizing with the enemy and earning strange looks from the staff.

"Sounds good." Blake leaned back against the counter and looked over his notepad, making a few notations here and there.

Zoe moved off, determined to act like everything was normal. Even though around Blake, nothing was normal anymore. Ten minutes later, her resolve to be strong was back in place.

She approached Blake. "I'm done and free to help if you need me.

"Of course. Four hands are better than two." Blake chuckled.

"Avoid clichés, mister. You've got it all wrong."

"I meant to. We certainly aren't putting our heads together on this, so my cliché works better."

"If you say so." Zoe shook her head and laughed.

Blake handed her one end of the tape measure. "I just need to make sure this is all to scale. Stand here and hold the tape at the edge of the counter, and I'll measure the width of the working area." All serious now, he walked away, the tape stretching between them. He pulled a little harder as he neared the glass case, the action popping the end out of her fingers, the metal tape furiously recoiling and snapping at the end. He shook his hand against the stinging pain.

Zoe winced. "I'm sorry. I should have held on tighter," she said, quick to apologize.

"I'll let it slide as I'm a big boy and it didn't hurt much. Just don't ever break my heart, as you pack a powerful punch, lady." Blake grinned, shooting her a wink.

"Not a chance. You don't have a heart to break." Zoe laughed, walking toward him to retrieve her end of the tape. He might put on a tough guy act, but she knew from experience how much it would have hurt.

"Ouch. Probably true, but when you put it like that..."

"You'll live. Like you said, you're a big boy and can handle it," she teased. Zoe didn't know where the confidence to joke with him this way was coming from. It had never been her strength. Witty repartee for her usually meant hours later she'd think of what she should have said and kick herself for not saying it.

The rest of the afternoon was spent working together, yet each one keeping their notes and drawings separate, not letting on to what they were doing. It was an odd situation to be sure, and one the other employees working commented on occasionally. By the time the team meeting rolled around, Zoe was ready. They met in the back room, out of earshot from the others who were working out front, Blake included.

Zoe stood in front of the small group. They all worked hard to help with ideas, and she hoped to make their dreams come true with a win and the bonus money. "All right, Team Zoe—this is it. Our final meeting. Before I go over everything we've decided and share some of the drawings so you can get a good feel for the final proposal I'll be submitting, does anyone have any questions?"

They looked at each other and shrugged. Something was amiss, she could sense it in the way they stood there, as if not entirely relaxed.

"Comments then?" Zoe asked. "You all seem like there's something on your mind."

More looks passed between the others. "Okay, I'll speak up for the group seeing as no one else is willing," Lindsey said. "For the past two days and even some before that, you and Mack Peterson's grandson have been pretty cozy. It doesn't take a genius to see the sparks flying between you and Blake. You even sat in church together. It's like you're playing both sides. We keep teasing you about it, but the reality is, we're worried."

Zoe let out a deep breath. She'd been afraid of this. "We're friends. There's nothing more than that between us." The competition was important. And for so many more reasons than the money. It was her future. Hers and Scotts. The team was right, her focus had been off, and it was something she needed to fix. At least until Saturday when this was all over.

"It just doesn't look that way to everyone who sees you two together," Lindsey said, shaking her head in disagreement. "It's all over town that Blake took Scott fishing. He told his buddies at school, who then told their parents, who then told everyone in town."

Zoe winced. She'd forgotten about the gossip chain in Hallbrook. "I'm sorry. He took Scott for the day so I could work here. That's all there was to it." At least they didn't know about the fireside hot beverage or the dinner they'd shared. *Or the kisses*. She'd never hear the end of it, and having her team's confidence was important to her.

"I promise I'm committed to winning the contest. I don't know what else to tell you."

"Fine. Just keep it that way. There's a lot of money on the line, and an opportunity like this may not come our way again," Tony said, throwing in his two cents.

"I get it. Let's go over the designs, and you all can be the judge if these are spectacular or whether you think I can do better." She only hoped they saw the beauty of what she'd put together and her vision for the creamery. Talking about Blake wouldn't serve any purpose, especially with the object of the discussion on the other side of the swinging door and apt to come through it at any time.

Chapter Seventeen

♥

THE PORSCHE STARTED RIGHT up. Blake said a silent prayer of gratitude. So far, he'd not had any other problem with it starting, leaving him to wonder if the mechanic was right and he'd not done something properly. It wouldn't be like him, but with all the distractions, and, of course, learning about the contest—anything was possible.

The meeting with Tammy Minton had been rescheduled for today at nine a.m., and Blake didn't want to be late or show up in his grandfather's old truck. He hadn't seen Tammy since high school, after she left town and married the Glen Haven quarterback. She was divorced now, or so he'd learned when he called the state inspector's office only to find out it was her.

If he'd known her identity in advance, he might not have asked her to meet him. But there was no way to wiggle out of it after he'd jumped in headfirst and issued the invitation. Tammy had been a case of getting what you think you want only to realize you were wrong all along. After she'd broken it off with him, he'd been relieved. She'd been a poor substitute for the girl he'd really wanted to date, except Zoe was off-limits. *Then and now.*

So why was he still attracted to her? Something he'd long ago figured as a childhood crush and something he'd outgrown. Hanging around her now had proven it was a lie.

Today's visit with Tammy was strictly business. Details, codes, logistics. All important things he needed to know to make sure every aspect of his proposal was on point and within the building codes set forth for Hallbrook. Zoe lived in town and had a distinct advantage of knowing the local regulations, something he needed a refresher course on and something Tammy could provide.

He pulled up in front of Peterson's and slid out of the car. Tammy was waiting in front of the shop, her cream-colored peacoat was buttoned up tight, and her fancy green and white scarf blowing in the chilly wind. "Good morning. I'm glad you could meet with me." Blake reached out to shake her gloved hand.

Tammy flashed him a smile, her red lips parting to reveal pearly white perfect teeth. Nothing but the best for her. She always had been daddy's little girl. "You knew I'd meet you, even if only for old times' sake. I was surprised when you called considering, ummm, our past. I'm sorry if I hurt you with the breakup."

"It's all in the past. Don't give it another thought." Blake hadn't, that's for sure. Unless it was to consider his lucky escape. Tammy was far too into herself and her own importance. Although, he would have never guessed she'd become a building inspector for the state. Her math and science skills weren't all that great, but socializing, now that was a subject she would have aced. Her father would have had to pull a few strings to make something like this happen, unless, of course, she'd changed. A lot.

"Let's get inside, shall we?" she asked, grabbing his arm and tucking her hand there. He didn't want to offend her and let the gesture stand.

They moved up the steps, and he pushed the door open, stepping back to let her pass first, thereby forcing her to drop the hold she had on him. Blake removed his coat and hung it up on the coat rack, Tammy following suit. He turned, only to discover Zoe watching their entrance.

Had she seen the arm holding? Not that it mattered. It's not like he and Zoe were dating, and he owed her no explanation. But then why did it seem wrong? Blake shoved the thought aside.

"Good morning, Zoe. You remember Tammy Wright, don't you? She's from the state building inspector's office. I invited her here to go over some of the rules and regulations to make sure I'm not designing anything that can't be implemented."

Tammy stepped forward, not one to hang back. "Hello, Zoe. It's wonderful to see you again," she gushed effusively.

"Of course, I remember her. Most popular girl in school." Blake swore there was a tinge of distaste in the tone of Zoe's voice, leaving him to wonder why.

"It's Minton now, although I am divorced. My marriage to Gary simply didn't work out for me, and Daddy took care of making it permanent. Such a blessing to be free of the odious man." The bracelets on her arms jangled as she exaggerated her words and pushed a lock of hair behind her ear. A practiced move, he recalled, designed to show off her neck and the jewels she wore.

"Good to see you again. Your father has his hands in a lot of pies around Hallbrook. I imagine his law firm could handle about anything you needed. You're lucky to have such a connection." The words were coming out of her mouth, a smiling mouth no less.

Blake was more certain than ever they weren't meant as a compliment. Wade Wright was a hotshot around town, but Blake had forgotten he had a law practice. Perhaps Zoe had been on the negative receiving end of his services. "We should get to work. I promise we won't get in your way." He wouldn't subject Zoe to Tammy any longer than necessary.

"Take your time. I'm sure you and Tammy have lots to catch up on." Zoe turned and walked away. Blake did a double-take.

Jealousy.

That's exactly what he saw in Zoe; the question was, why?

She had nothing to worry about from Tammy, and as far as she was concerned, him. Sure, he'd kissed her a few times. Innocent kisses that didn't promise a relationship or a future. Even if he had been thinking about Zoe often, or the fact he cared about her. A lot. Maybe more, but it wasn't anything he'd let himself name.

Relationships weren't his thing, but this one country-fresh and sweet minx seemed to have left her mark. Zoe wasn't like the usual women he went on dates with, which was an even bigger reason to steer clear. Zoe would want it all, and truth be told, Blake wanted her to find happiness. Just not with him. Or so he tried to convince himself.

"Blake, darling, why don't we start over here." She took his arm again and led him behind the counter.

"Sure thing," he said, pulling his arm away to get his tape measure. "What's the recommended minimum distance between the back and front counters?"

"Three feet is minimum, but with the traffic flow and the number of employees you have, I'd suggest moving the cases out to forty-two inches. Less chance for accidents. It meets the old code, but if you do a complete renovation, you'll need to move it out to meet the new code, It will need to include the ADA regulations since you have more than fourteen employees. You'll also need to make sure you have wheelchair access thirty-six inches wide from the door to the ordering counter and register, and the counter no more than thirty-four inches in height. The area for the customer should be thirty inches long by forty-eight inches wide to allow for a wheel-chair bound individual complete access to the creamery and the ability to maneuver."

Blake was surprised. It would seem Tammy had changed because one thing was for certain, she knew her stuff. "That would cut us down a few tables, but I'm sure I can make it work. The design I'm working on is more streamline contemporary and the seating takes up far less room."

"You always were smart in school. I'm sure you'll have the perfect designs to win this competition. Maybe we could go to dinner this evening and discuss them further. I'd love to hear your ideas." She smiled up at him, her red lips parted as she batted her eyelashes.

Good grief. Not in this lifetime—or in the lifetime after the first time out with her. "Tonight's not a good night. I'm sorry. The designs are due tonight and I'll need every minute to finish them. Thanks anyway," he said, glancing over at Zoe, hoping she hadn't overheard Tammy's invitation.

No such luck.

She shook her head and shot him a dirty look. He had no idea she'd started to care for him this much, but her responses couldn't be for any other reason. Blake rather liked this feisty side of her and couldn't wait to finish up with Tammy so he could tease Zoe about it.

Zoe couldn't believe Blake had shown up this morning with Tammy Minton. She didn't care what her last name was now; the fact remained she was Wade Wright's daughter. A man who was a prominent member of Carney & Wright law firm, and someone who just happened to also be a member of the town council. How dare he bring her here and then laugh and joke like they were best friends?

Tammy's high, lilting voice had carried the dinner invitation to Zoe's ears. Not that she'd heard Blake's answer. And not that it mattered. Tammy's connection to a contest judge was too close. Zoe had returned to the back office, begrudging every minute that Tammy spent with Blake. The woman's flirty smiles and laughter had been all too obvious she wanted to reconnect with her old high school flame.

An hour passed, and Zoe hadn't done a thing. Sneaking out the back door, she ran to the post office to drop off some of the bills she'd paid this morning.

"Oomph," she exhaled, running smack dab into someone. "I'm so sorry, Mr. Blevins." Lost deep in thought, she hadn't seen Walter coming out of the building.

"Where you off to in such a hurry, Zoe?" he asked, not letting go of her arm until he was sure she wouldn't topple over.

"Nowhere. Just thinking when I should be paying attention to where I'm walking." Zoe laughed, trying to make a joke at her expense. It was the easiest way to brush off the embarrassment. It suddenly occurred to her that Mr. Blevins was another member of the council. One of the oldest, and therefore, one that would know and love the creamery and have memories of the past. Or at least she hoped. It could be fate she'd literally run into him. If Blake could cross the lines with Miss Social Butterfly, Zoe could talk to Mr. Blevins. It was only fair.

"Okay, then. You have a nice day," he said, tipping his hat.

"Wait. I wanted to talk to you about something," Zoe said in a rush, not wanting to miss this opportunity to get a feel for things.

"What's that?" He paused and turned back, coming to stand next to her.

"I was just wondering, you know, like what good memories you have at the ice cream shop? I want to make sure I've incorporated ideas that capture the imagination of days gone by. Can you tell me some of your favorites?" Code for *remember what you loved about the place and don't let Blake come in and rip it all away.*

"This is all about the contest, isn't it?" he asked, his brow furrowing a bit.

Zoe flushed red. Of course, it was. "In a way," she said, hedging her answer. I've finished the designs but was hoping to get a sense of what you loved best about the creamery." There was no way she could tell him the truth. What she really wanted was to see where his vote would land. Did he favor *on with the old,* or was he an *in with the new* kind of voter. Zoe knew she shouldn't have asked. If Blake wanted to be unethical, it was his problem, but she didn't need to do likewise. "Forget I asked. It's crossing a line considering the contest results will be announced tomorrow."

Mr. Blevins smiled. "I'm glad to hear you retract your question. You always were a good girl and I'd hate to think you'd try to use an old geezer like me to get an edge. Not that I would have told you anything." He chuckled, tipped his hat, and strode off down the steps.

She'd be glad when the competition was over. Zoe headed back to the creamery, thrilled to discover little Miss Social Butterfly had left.

Blake came around the corner and met her at the door, the grin on his face unsettling.

"Did you need something?" she asked, trying to keep her own tone businesslike.

He leaned in close. "I noticed something earlier this morning and I wanted to ask you about it." His grin widened.

The more he grinned, the tenser she got. Was his good mood the result of Tammy's efforts to lure him into her clutches? Or worse, the other way around. "What's that? I don't have all day to stand around chatting," she said frostily.

"Are you mad at me?" What was his first clue?

"Why would I be mad?" Spitting mad, to be exact, not that she'd tell him.

"When Tammy was here, I got the sense you were jealous, perhaps?" His brows shot up a notch, his grin now stretching from ear to ear.

Zoe closed her eyes for a second and tried to breathe. Blake was beyond belief. "Talk about conceited. Jealous—hardly. Who you choose to hang out with is none of my business. I'd just prefer it to be after the contest before you went on a date. It's a little unethical, don't you think?" she snapped.

The grin slipped from his face as deep lines set in across his forehead. "What do you mean, unethical? She's a building inspector, not a judge."

"You've got some nerve. Do you really expect me to believe you don't know?"

"Know what, Zoe?" Blake pressed, taking a step toward her. "Tell me what's going on."

"That her daddy is on the town council, and therefore—a judge."

Blake paled. She had to give him credit; he did act surprised by the news. But acting surprised didn't mean it wasn't part of an act. Zoe started to walk away, not wanting to discuss it. His lack of integrity had almost cost her hers, something she would have never forgiven herself for.

Blake grabbed her arm to stop her from leaving. "Zoe, I had no idea. You must believe me. And for the record, I know you heard her ask me out, but you should also know my answer was no." She believed him, the remorse in his expression real.

"Fine. I believe you." It just didn't change anything. And that's where the real problem lay—it had been there all along; she'd just tried to ignore it. Zoe had been kidding herself to believe she'd ever had a shot against Mack Peterson's grandson. The old man was having his fun, but just like most of the employees had chosen his side, Zoe knew their reasoning was sound. Blake was sure he would win, and the problem was, so did she. "I've got to finish some paperwork. See you later." She walked away, and this time Blake let her go.

Maybe it was time to start putting out some feelers for a new job. Come tomorrow, she was sure she'd lose, and without the manager's job after all these years of working here, it would be time to admit it was a dead-end job and time to do something different for her and Scott's future.

Chapter Eighteen

♥

"SCOTT, ARE YOU ABOUT ready to go? We don't want to be late," Zoe hollered down the hall.

"Coming, Mom. Just getting my sneakers on," Scott yelled back.

Tapping her foot on the hardwood floor, the sound was like the echo of her heart thumping in her chest. Today was a big day, and though she was almost certain Blake would ultimately be named the winner, until it happened, she was still in the running and there was still a chance for her to take the next step in her career. The money would come in handy, and after years of scrimping, it would be a huge blessing to her and Scott.

But first, they had to get to the Easter dinner festivities at the Peterson's. Her son came trudging down the hall, looking spiffy in his khaki slacks and cream cable-knit sweater. The sneakers were sort of a bargaining tool to get him to dress up for an event in a barn—a compromise of sorts to get him to go willingly.

Zoe tossed him his jacket. "It'll be fun. There are always other kids to play with and you know it."

"But I want to go to Devon's. We had plans to play Mario racing. It was my turn to pick which car and driver I wanted to be first." Scott's sullen expression wasn't a good addition to Zoe's already frazzled nerves.

"I'm sure Devon will let you go first next time. Besides, you never know, Blake will be there. Maybe if you ask him, you can play with Hank a little bit." Of course, there was no telling what the rest of the day held for either one of them, but it was worth a shot to improve her son's attitude.

"Really? Cool." Scott's smile returned as he pulled on his jacket and zipped it up.

Zoe drove the short distance to the Peterson Dairy Farm on the other side of town. The parking lot was full already, but then some people were there for the public skating Mack Peterson offered on his rink. The employee party at the barn was a private affair, but afterward, many would take advantage of the rink to burn off excess calories consumed at the huge dinner Old Man Peterson catered in.

Zoe pulled open the barn door, the warmth, soft lighting, and country music spilling out. It was all quite welcoming. She pulled off her scarf and hat and looked around. Team Zoe stood gathered together talking amongst themselves, their families nowhere in sight.

"Look, Scott, there's Jeff from your class and some other kids playing games over there," she suggested, pointing to the corner set up for kid's games. The Peterson's employees numbered close to fifty or sixty and with all their families; the place was packed.

"Okay, see ya," Scott said, running off, his Mario troubles a thing of the past.

Zoe smiled and headed toward her team, intent on talking to them. They were all keyed up and nervous about the announcement. Everyone on her team had given a hundred and fifty percent in their efforts and she was proud of them, no matter the outcome. The four of them had grown closer and she'd learned more about their knowledge and skills way beyond what she'd known prior to the contest. Even their hesitations about her and Blake's blossoming friendship hadn't changed anything in the end. They knew she wanted to win.

"Hey, everyone. Anyone sleep last night?" she teased. She, herself, had tossed and turned all night, worried about the outcome but still willing to pray for the best. Over and over.

"Are you kidding? I even dreamed of today and filled in the blanks the way I wanted them to end," Lindsey said, the excitement in her voice matching Zoe's.

"That would be exhausting." Zoe grinned, shaking her head.

"It was, but totally worth it." Lindsey laughed. "At least I know what to say and do if it happens."

"Do?" Zoe asked, unsure what she meant.

"Dance. You know, a happy dance," Lindsey added, doing a three-sixty for added emphasis.

"And I'll dance with you," Tony said, his gaze squarely fixed on Lindsey. If Chad didn't step up soon, Tony would sweep Lindsey off her feet before he got the nerve up to ask her out.

"Can I have your attention, please?" Old Man Peterson called out from the front of the barn where they'd set up a stage. "I know you're all excited to hear the results of the contest."

The excitement in the room rose higher as everyone involved agreed.

"But," he said, holding up his hand. "I reckon we should have dinner first. It's our annual Peterson family Easter dinner, and we should give thanks for all the blessings each and every one of us have in our lives. In the early days, we used to have every employee say what they were thankful for the most that year, but we've grown into such a big family, I fear we'd be here until the rooster crows come morning." Mack chuckled, everyone nodding in agreement and laughing with him. "Especially with Charlie here. Our mayor is a bit long-winded." Mack smiled at Charlie, who waved off the teasing good-naturedly as the crowd continued to laugh.

Zoe and the others made their way to one of the long tables and took a seat at the end. She laid her jacket on the chair next to her for Scott and looked for him, hoping he'd heard the announcement and was already headed her way.

A hand landed on her shoulder, making her jump. She spun around. *Blake.*

She wished he'd quit doing that; it made her look like a nervous wreck. Although, in this instance, she was.

"Hey, there. I just wanted to wish you luck," Blake said, giving her shoulder a gentle squeeze.

"You too. It's just a contest, and the better design will win. I'm okay with the results either way." It sounded good. She'd rehearsed the line somewhere in the middle of the night should the opportunity present itself. Taking a high road when you were sure to get the short road wasn't easy, but it was the right thing to do.

"Thanks. I had fun working with you and appreciate your help teaching me the ropes around the creamery. It was an eye-opening experience for sure." Blake's warm smile curled her toes. Now wasn't the time to be tripping over her own emotions.

"Hey, Blake, did you bring Hank?" Scott asked, coming up beside her and sliding into his seat.

"Good to see you again, Scott. And I'm sorry, but no, I didn't bring him. I was afraid he'd get into mischief with all the food around and lots of people wanting to feed him table scraps when he started begging."

"Okay," her son said, a little of the luster going out of him.

"I'm sure after the meal and the announcements, if your mom is willing, I can take you up to the house to see him for a few minutes. He'll be anxious to get out and have a run." Blake seemed to zero in on Scott's desire to play with the dog and offered up the perfect solution.

"Can I, Mom? Can I?" Scott asked.

"Sure." Zoe laughed, knowing she'd not refuse her son a bit of fun. After all, she'd pulled him away from a night of Mario racing.

"Yes!" Scott exclaimed, giving Blake a high five.

"Just for a few minutes, as we've got to get home afterward and get to bed. Easter sunrise service comes early."

"Are you coming to the service?" Scott asked Blake, her son's happy smile back in place. Sooner or later, she'd have to get the kid a dog. But life needed to be more settled, so now wasn't the time.

"I hadn't given it any thought, but maybe. I'll see what I can do about joining you both," Blake said, the last part directed at her.

"That would be lovely." Okay, so maybe her niceness was now topping into the sickly-sweet category.

Blake shot her an odd look. "Team Blake saved me a seat down toward the other end of the table and I should join them."

"Drats. I was hoping you could sit with us," Scott said, more proof of the tight bond the two shared.

"Sorry, buddy. I'll find you after the announcement is made. I promise." Blake made his way to his seat just as Old Man Peterson signaled for everyone to quiet down.

After asking the blessing, he signaled for the caterers to begin serving. The place became a flurry of activity as a plateful of food was delivered to every person in attendance. Ham topped with a pineapple ring and a cherry in the center. Potatoes. Peas. Squash. Cranberry jelly. Coleslaw. And loads of orange sauce in a gravy boat for people to drown the meat to their heart's content. She knew from experience, the pecan pie and chocolate torte served for dessert would be divine and she'd need to not overeat.

Scott dug in, his appetite matching his enthusiasm to see the dog later tonight.

The conversation remained light, everyone as if by mutual agreement, avoiding the competition as a topic. Nerves and anticipation were running high as another hour passed before Old Man Peterson stepped back up to the microphone.

"Now that your bellies are full, I think it's time to make our announcement. For those present that haven't heard about it, a competition was set up two weeks ago at Peterson's Ice Creamery. Team Zoe and Team Blake were formed, with all the employees having to choose one team to join. Each team was tasked with designing a plan for the renovation of the shop as I feel it's time to fix up the place."

The silence in the room stretched her emotions tighter. Only the sound of a crying child in the back or an occasional cough could be heard. "I'd like to call the two teams up to the stage. All of you."

One by one, Zoe, the staff, and Blake, made their way to the front, dividing themselves into their teams.

"Blake is with Modern Designs Inc, a high-tech corporation and he has wonderful insights for technologically advanced ideas. Zoe, on the other hand, is quite old-fashioned, preferring a more nostalgic touch. Both teams turned in their design plans yesterday to the town council, and last night, we came to a decision based on votes cast by the council, my son, Robert, and myself. So, without further ado, I'd like to congratulate...Team...Zoe."

Old Man Peterson's smiling face was looking at her, and she could have sworn he said Team Zoe. As the whoops and hollers of the rest of her team reached her ears, they pulled her in for a group hug and started dancing. It was then the information sank in.

They'd won. Against all odds—Team Zoe was the winner

She felt bad for Blake and his team, glancing in their direction. The dejected looks on their faces robbed her of some of the joy. She wished they could all be winners, but unfortunately, someone had to lose. It was Blake's expression that caused her the most grief. Whether it because of the pain she saw hidden in the depths of his eyes, or her own feelings for him, she wasn't sure.

"As part of the winning package, I'd like to name Zoe Carruthers as the new manager of Peterson's Ice Creamery. She's been working here for the most part since she was sixteen, and I can't think of a better person to take on the role. The entire team will receive a cash bonus for their efforts in helping her put together a sound proposal that I feel the town will love. Zoe will also oversee the renovations to the shop which I've scheduled to begin at the first of the month. The creamery will be closed for two weeks, and we'll have a grand reopening at that point, and I hope you'll join us for the celebration."

Loud cheers and clapping came from the audience as Mack came up and shook each person's hand. Zoe noticed the others had left the stage to leave her team the spotlight and to bask in their success. It was a moment she'd never forget.

The only downside was Blake. His ideas were good, just not for one of Hallbrook's landmarks. For Zoe, the shop and the chance to manage it were her life. Blake, on the other hand, was already doing quite well for himself. He'd leave town and go back to his posh apartment and city job.

Sneaking another glance in his direction, the tense expression hadn't lessened. Zoe's gaze lingered; her emotions conflicted. It must have hurt, losing like this, especially because of the family connection. The results of today would always be between her and Blake, ending any blossoming friendship. They'd known all along this day would come; they just didn't know how it would end.

Scott ran up to her, joining in the group hug. "You won, Mom."

"Yes, honey, we won. And guess what else?" she said, kneeling next to him.

"What?" he asked, catching on to her excitement.

It was the moment she'd longed to give her son, and now, finally, she could say the words. "We're going to Disney World."

Scott's eyes grew wide, his mouth hanging open in stunned surprise. A hopeful look sprang up on his face as if he wasn't sure if he'd heard her correctly. "You mean it? Really and truly? We're going to Disney World?"

Her eyes blurred as tears pooled. "Really and truly," she said, pulling him in for a hug. "Right after the renovations are finished, you, me, and Sarah are going on a vacation."

"Yippee," he exclaimed, doing his own version of a happy dance.

Chapter Nineteen

♥

"SORRY, EVERYONE. WE TRIED, but it simply wasn't enough to sway the old-timers in town," Blake said, although he knew his father was one of the votes against them, and nothing would have changed his mind.

"I really thought we'd win. So much for my new home theater system." Chad shook his head, disappointed Team Blake lost.

"Someone had to lose, just never thought it would be us," Keith chimed in.

"For the record, I think we did a great job, and I couldn't have been more pleased with everyone's contribution to the project. Enjoy the rest of the evening and try not to dwell on the outcome. I'm going to talk to some people here, seeing as I won't be in town much longer."

"Yeah, not much choice in the matter," Brenda agreed. For a quiet person, her sullen expression more than conveyed her emotions.

Blake moved off, spotting one of the council members standing by themselves. "Hey, Fred. What's up?" Blake asked the older man as he approached him.

"Just getting older day by day." Fred chuckled. "Tough loss today. I think you had some great ideas, but your dad is set in his ways and so are some of the other council members. Crotchety, if you ask me. I may be old, but I'm not dead, and I like to shake things up now and then." Fred grabbed a cookie off the tray the caterer offered and bit into it.

"I figured as much with my dad. Sometimes, I think it's more about me than my ideas that he's resisting. He hates that I'm not following in his footsteps and that I choose designing over farming." Blake had known this for a long time but now, as he got older did the reality start to bother him.

Fred nodded. "He's a tough nut to crack, but I'm not telling you anything you don't know."

"Thanks for your support though." Fred's earlier response confirmed what he suspected regarding the older man's vote. He couldn't help but be curious who'd joined his grandfather and father against his ideas.

"No problem, just sorry it didn't work out for you. What will you do now?" Fred asked, finishing off his cookie.

"Head back to the city. I've got to catch up on my work and drum up some new projects. Modern Designs has been great letting me work from here for a bit, but it's time to go back."

"Try not to wait so long before you return. Your grandpa misses you." Fred clapped him on the back.

"I know. But I also realize now he never intended to vote against my dad. The odds were stacked in Zoe's favor. My ideas were good, but not good enough to sway enough of the others. So much for progress in Hallbrook."

"I would have thought Wade Wright had more pull, but a five-four vote against you is still a loss. Tough luck."

An elderly man approached. "Hey, Fred, I think Mary was looking for you a minute ago. Reckon you better go find your wife," he said, grinning.

"Absolutely. Don't want to be in the doghouse tonight." Fred chuckled. "See you later, Blake. Don't forget what I told you about coming back here."

"I won't. Thanks for the heads up." *And thanks for all the other information.* With a four-four vote, his grandfather had been the tiebreaker and he'd voted against Blake. It was seriously disappointing after all he'd put into the designs.

Blake scanned the room in search of Wade to thank him for his support. Connections were good in his line of work. The only positive to the whole thing was that with his loss, Zoe won. He didn't begrudge her the success and promotion that came with it. He'd watched how hard she worked for the past two weeks and how much she was responsible for. It was a miracle she hadn't left for greener pastures a while ago. Now, she wouldn't have to.

The other miracle was that he felt the way he did, something that didn't make any sense. It was a contest and he'd lost—so why was he happy for her? And why did the thought of leaving Hallbrook cause his heart to feel heavy?

Zoe. Or more like not seeing her every day. And then there was Scott. The kid hadn't liked him at first, but now they were buddies. Blake's level of satisfaction had increased exponentially having Scott look up to him. It was like he was making a difference in the kid's life, and it felt good.

And right now, Scott was coming in his direction. Blake remembered his promise to take him to visit Hank. "Can we go now?" Scott asked.

"Let's just stop by and let your mom know," Blake said. "Wouldn't want her to worry." They headed in her direction, and she stepped away from the group she was talking to when she noticed them approaching.

"Congratulations to you and your team. Well done," Blake said, taking the high road and wanting her to know he was happy for her success.

Zoe's gentle smile was his reward. "Thank you. It came as quite a shock."

"I'm sure. Somehow, you were convinced I was going to win. It's nice to see you were finally wrong about something." Blake chuckled, trying to keep the discussion light and not a reflection of his own inner turmoil.

"And we're going to Disney World," Scott said, his eyes wide and a beaming grin on his face.

Blake loved the kid's enthusiasm, and it made Zoe's win all the more relevant. "That's awesome. Sound like a good time, for sure."

"Maybe you could come with us?" Scott asked, the innocence of the question startling. For a kid who positively didn't want Blake near his mother, the boy had done a complete one-eighty.

Blake shook his head. "It doesn't work that way, buddy. And I've got to go back to the city to my job."

"Do you have to go? What about our fishing trip?" Scott asked, his face scrunched up, not liking the idea of him leaving.

"I'll be back when I can. I did promise, after all."

"Or better yet," Zoe said, laying her hand on his arm, "why don't you stick around and help me do the renovations? I can hire you as a consultant, and you can keep working from home on your other projects. It's a win-win situation." Only Zoe would think to ask him to help her, generosity and kindness her middle name.

"Thanks, but no thanks. I've overstayed my welcome and I'm going back to the city to a company that appreciates my ideas and insights. Peterson's has once again proven to me I was right to leave in the first place." Apparently, the fact it was a family business meant nothing to his father or grandfather. His father—he understood. They'd always been at odds. But his grandfather? That's what hurt. Especially given he'd asked Blake to come in the first place, giving him hope things were changing.

"Sorry to hear that. I'll miss seeing you every day," Zoe said, her voice soft and genuine.

And more emotional than Blake wanted. "Or maybe secretly relieved I'll be out of your hair," he teased.

Zoe grinned. "Hardly that. It wasn't all bad, you know. In fact, most of it was rather enjoyable."

Blake couldn't remember any parts he didn't like. "True." His gaze slid to her mouth. One part, in particular, he really enjoyed, as he remembered the first kiss they'd shared. It wasn't looking like there would be a repeat on the menu.

A loud tapping sounded on the nearby speakers. Blake looked up to the stage area to see his grandfather getting ready to speak.

"I know folks are about to leave or head over to the skating rink, but before you all go, I've got one last announcement to make." The room fell silent as everyone stopped talking and turned their attention to him. "I was waiting until after Team Zoe had a chance for a much-deserved celebration of the win, but I have another big announcement no one is expecting, but one that is certainly long overdue. Blake, can you come up here, please?"

Blake shot a glance at Zoe, unsure what this was about. She shrugged, nodding in the direction of the stage.

"I'll be right back, Scott. I don't have a clue what he's up to," Blake added, wondering about this new development.

He made his way to the front and stood next to his grandfather.

"As you all know, my grandson, Blake, is a tech design expert in modernization and efficiency planning. His designs were fantastic that he submitted for the contest, but in all fairness, the only thing they failed to take into account was our small town and the folks who live here every day. Sometimes, it's not about profit. It's about making memories and having traditions.

"After much thought and since all final decisions rest with me with regards to the Peterson Corporation, I'd like to announce a new position within the company. Blake," his grandfather said, turning to him, "you're talented and have great foresight that Peterson's could use. And as a family-owned and operated business, it gives me great pleasure to offer you the position of Chief Technology Officer. As CTO, you will have full control over all technology designs within the corporation and report directly to me. I think it's high time the farms were modernized, and the talents of our employees more greatly utilized."

Blake hadn't seen this coming and was momentarily speechless.

His grandfather reached out to shake his hand. "I hope your silence is a stunned silence and not a negative answer." The old man laughed, knowing all Blake ever wanted was to become a valuable part of the family business and to be respected for his innovative ideas.

"Let's go with stunned," Blake said, grinning and accepting the handshake. *Finally, he was home to stay.* "I accept the position whole-heartedly." Everyone in the barn burst into a round of applause and hooted and hollered country style.

"And I'd like to offer my official congratulations to Team Zoe on behalf of the company. Also, to let you know that this means I'll need to see your designs to go over them before they're finalized. Sounds like I have the rubber stamp of approval," he said, laughing as he shot her a teasing grin.

Except she didn't look happy. No smile. Just a deer-caught-in-the-headlights sort of look.

Blake and his grandfather stepped off the stage. Lots of well-wishers came up to congratulate him. When a short reprise came about, he leaned over to his grandfather in order to be heard. "Thanks again. I look forward to talking with you more about this, but I've got to go take care of something. You won't be disappointed with what I can bring to the company, I promise."

"I know. That's why I wanted you home. The contest was just to shake you up a bit and see what you could do. I wanted to know your level of commitment, and I must say, I'm proud of you." His grandfather shook his head and smiled.

"Too bad Dad didn't feel the same," Blake quipped.

"I'll talk to him. Trust me, he'll come around. He's hardworking and set in his ways. More so than me at that age, which isn't a bad thing sometimes. But right now, I'd like to see Peterson's grow and continue to help the community any way we can."

"Sounds like a plan. Can we talk later?" Blake asked.

His grandfather eyed him curiously. "Where you off to in such a rush?"

"I promised to take Scott Carruthers over to play with Hank for a little bit. The two are pretty close, and Scott's eager to get a dog of his own. This helps Zoe in the interim."

"I see. Speaking of close, what's going on with you and Zoe? Any chance with you moving back to town, you might actually act on your interest?

She's a great gal," his grandfather said, a jovial expression on his face.

Blake shrugged. "I agree with you about the great gal part. I'm just not sure I'm the romantic type. Never have been, and you know it." Lately, he wasn't so sure. And moving back to Hallbrook for good, complicated things even further. Staying in town meant seeing more of Zoe.

"Everyone's the romantic type; it's just some it takes a little longer to find the right woman. I reckon if you give it a chance, you might find you'd met your match in her."

"Grandpa, stop with the matchmaking." He was having a hard enough time dealing with emotions on his own without the added pressure to push him in a direction he previously avoided.

"Well, your sister seems to think there's something going on between you." His grandfather's grin had widened, his eyes twinkling in merriment.

At one point, she was against him spending time with Zoe when they were younger, and more recently, she'd read him the riot act after the kiss she'd witnessed. He couldn't imagine what she was telling others. "What'd she say?" Blake asked.

"Something about a kiss and some other nonsense about you going out with the wrong women, but I reckon that part I shouldn't be telling." He chuckled.

"Who I date is my own business. And the kiss Sarah saw was nothing more than a birthday kiss." Blake was defending his own actions, even though the words were a lie. But the more people who knew the truth, the more they would push him in Zoe's direction.

"And you haven't kissed her since then?" His grandfather shook his head. "You sure are a slow one to figure things out when it comes to women than you are with your fast technological ideas."

"I never said I didn't," Blake countered before realizing what he was admitting to.

His grandfather laughed. "I reckon your sister was right then."

"Grandpa." He was going to wring Sarah's neck—and find out what rumors she'd been spreading.

"You go on and see your Zoe."

"It's Scott," Blake insisted, but he was talking to thin air, his grandfather already walking away.

Tammy came rushing up to him, wrapping her arms around his neck. "Congratulations, Blake. What a great job offer." She leaned in toward him, Blake was unable to turn away quick enough to avoid her kiss. "You deserved to win the contest as well, but some members of the council just wouldn't be swayed."

He stepped out of her reach, barely able to resist wiping his mouth. It wasn't Tammy's kisses he wanted. "Thank you. Zoe won fair and square, and the job offer is way better. I'll have control over the entire modernization of the Peterson corporation. I'm looking forward to the challenge and to moving home." Blake tried to keep the conversation centered on business.

"I'm sure you'll be great at it," Tammy gushed, laying her hand on his arm.

"Thanks. I've got to talk to some other people here but enjoy the rest of your evening." Tammy looked a little put out, but she'd survive.

Blake started across the room, searching the area where he'd left Zoe, but they were nowhere in sight. "Hey, Chad. Have you seen Zoe and Scott?"

"They left not long ago. Scott didn't seem to happy about it, but I remember as a kid, I hated it when the fun ended." Chad smiled.

Only in this case, Scott's fun wasn't supposed to end. Why would Zoe leave knowing he'd promised her son a visit to see Hank? Blake recalled her expression after the announcement. She hadn't been happy, and less so with his teasing remark. He would have thought she'd have been overjoyed, considering her earlier offer for him to stick around town and work with her.

It would seem the only destiny the two of them shared would to never be on the same page.

Chapter Twenty

❤

S COTT HADN'T GONE QUIETLY from the party Saturday night, leaving Zoe to feel guilty for making him go home. Blake's promise to let Scott play with Hank had been the driving factor in her son's attitude, and her own lame excuse about not feeling well hadn't been enough for him to forgive her for wanting to leave in a hurry. It hadn't been fair to Scott, but it had been for the best. Sometimes, disappointment came in various shapes and sizes, and both she and Scott had a healthy dose of it last night.

Zoe wanted time to think things through and to put her emotions on lockdown. At the party, three major revelations occurred to her, all within minutes of each other. One, Blake would be her new boss, which could change her plans for the renovation. Two, the hug and kiss she'd witnessed Tammy lay on Blake were not by any stretch of the imagination congratulatory. What Zoe saw was way more friendly than what Blake had let on. Third, and by far the worse, Zoe realized her feelings for Blake ran far deeper than she'd been willing to admit.

Love. Finally, she had a word to identify the closeness she'd shared with him. There was no way she could stick around and face Blake, knowing what she knew. Thinking time had been in order before they met up again. Time to allow her to compartmentalize her emotions.

Sunday morning came super early after a sleepless night. The sunrise Easter service had been especially beautiful and peaceful. There was no sign of Blake, although his father and grandfather were there. It was for the better, considering she was no closer to knowing what to say to him.

Hey, congratulations, and oh, by the way, I've fallen in love with you. Or, congratulations, I see you got the job and the girl. Tammy must be thrilled you're back together. No, that sounded far too jealous. The ugly truth was, it sounded that way because she was jealous. Not a pretty trait. Zoe shoved the conversation in her head to the far recesses and tried to focus on all the positives in her life.

She still had the promotion, the raise, and the bonus. And by the time she crawled into bed, she'd begun to wonder if perhaps she'd overreacted to Tammy's hug and kiss. One thing was for sure, she planned to ask him. Of course, that was if he showed up at the shop this morning. Zoe wasn't sure of his plans, but she'd find out all too soon.

With Scott at Devon's for the day, Zoe headed to the creamery. She was the first to arrive, but it wasn't long before the morning shift employees turned up. The conversation centered around the contest, with teasing remarks going back and forth between the two teams.

Zoe preferred to stay out of the mix but couldn't help smiling when Lindsey got in a few remarks, the girl a staunch believer the right team won. Of course, the bonus money was a sore subject for those that had mentally spent the money, assuming they would win. She knew the feeling of wanting something only to not get it. It's how she felt when she couldn't take Scott on vacation or wasn't being promoted to the job she deserved. Finally, it was her turn to have some of her dreams answered. The only one that wasn't working out would be the love she felt for Blake.

"I saw Blake out last night at O'Malley's. He didn't look overly upset with losing the contest if you ask me," Chad told Lindsey as the two set up the tables and booths for the day. Zoe leaned in toward the pair, Blake's name caught her attention.

"Well, he did get a really good job and it's right up his alley. What's he got to be upset about?" Lindsey asked, pausing from filling the napkin holder.

Zoe couldn't help but agree. She stopped mixing the batch of ice cream she was working on, not wanting to miss what was being said. She tried not to make it obvious she was listening, but when it came to Blake, she was all ears—and heart.

Chad laughed. "I think he got more than a new job."

"What's that mean?" Lindsey asked. If she hadn't, Zoe might have had to come out of hiding and ask the question herself.

"I heard he's gone back to the city to pack up and move his stuff here, but it looks like he's coming back to Hallbrook for a job *and* Tammy Minton. The two were awfully chummy last night if you know what I mean." Chad grinned.

Zoe's stomach clenched, a sick feeling washing over her.

"Oh, really? Someone said they dated in high school, but I didn't think he was interested the day she stopped in at the creamery."

"Things changed, I guess."

Change was an understatement. It was one thing when she suspected Blake was with Tammy but had rejected the notion without confirmation. Hearing they were out on a date was quite another. And as for talking to him face to face, it would seem that wouldn't happen anytime soon if he'd left town.

Blake and Tammy—together again.

"I guess so, but I sure don't seem her as his type. But she is the building inspector, so I suppose it's an advantageous relationship. Not to mention, her daddy has a lot of pull in town."

"Simply put, it's called greasing the wheels of change. And she's not bad to look at either." Chad laughed.

"Grow up," Lindsey said, shaking her head in disgust.

They moved on to talk about other things going on in town, and Zoe shut them out of her head. She didn't want to believe Chad, but there was no reason to doubt him. Forcing herself to focus, she finished the batch of Mint Chocolate Chip ice cream, deposited it in the freezer, and headed for her office.

The kind of thinking she needed to do was best done privately. Eavesdropping was never good, and this time, the old adage certainly applied. Knowing what she knew, there didn't seem to be a way for things to work out.

Larry had taught her a few things about the love 'em and leave 'em types of guys. Zoe wouldn't stand by and watch Blake with Tammy knowing it would rip her heart out, and even when Blake finally dumped her, there'd be no going back to the way things were. The best thing would be for her to leave Peterson's. *Move on.*

Zoe toyed with the idea of resigning but just as quickly shoved the notion aside. Not until she had proof would she give up everything she'd accomplished.

Five days later, Zoe still hadn't heard from Blake. Her bank account, on the other hand, was two thousand dollars richer in balance. Scott had eventually come around as the two spent their evenings planning the trip to Disney World.

With the money available, she even upgraded the plan to include staying at one of the onsite resorts. Five days and four nights of Florida sunshine. The countdown had started, her vacation time approved almost immediately by Mack Peterson. She'd picked the first week after the renovation was scheduled for completion. Scott had drawn a calendar, and each morning, he woke up to cross off another day, his excitement and discussions for what he wanted to see and do increasing daily.

The after-school customers were always higher on Fridays, and Zoe remained out front to lend a helping hand to the staff. She'd kept busy between coordinating the contractors all week, something that helped take her mind off Blake's absence. Next week, the place would close, and renovations would begin.

The bell jingled over the door announcing another arrival.

Tammy Minton.

Zoe headed for the backroom, determined to avoid the woman.

"Yoo-hoo, Zoe, wait," Tammy called out loud enough for all to hear, making it so Zoe had no choice but to stop.

She turned, pasting on a fake smile. "Hi, Tammy. What's up?" Not that she cared, but she was the manager, and the customer came first.

"I came in for some ice cream but was hoping to talk to you about something. Do you have a minute?" The woman's heavy perfume wafted her way, slightly choking.

Zoe nodded. "Sure thing. What did you want? I can have someone fix it while we chat."

"Thank you so much. A hot fudge sundae would be lovely." The woman's socialite princess act rubbed Zoe the wrong way. She preferred genuine people and couldn't imagine what Blake saw in her.

She turned to Lindsey. There was no mistaking the girl's undisguised interest in what was going on. "Can you get Tammy a hot fudge sundae while she and I talk for a minute? Oh, and I'll take a soda, please."

"Sure thing. I'll get right on it," Lindsey said.

"Let's sit over here," Zoe indicated, pointing to an available table, away from listening ears. "So, what's up? I only have a few minutes to spare before I need to run a deposit to the bank." It was Zoe's way of keeping the conversation short—a planned exit.

"Well, I'll get right to the point. Seeing as you're the new manager, I figured you should be in the loop." Tammy tapped her perfectly manicured and polished nails on the table.

"In the loop?" Zoe asked, more than a little confused. But then, the heavy perfume filling the air probably had something to do with it. Clearly, Tammy didn't know the word moderation.

"Yes, you know, about the upcoming renovation," Tammy said, acting as though the information were common knowledge.

As far as Zoe knew, the so-called loop involved her and Mack Peterson, and Blake to some extent. "I've got those under control."

"That may have been true at one point, but there are some changes that need to be addressed. Blake really wants this creamery to succeed and his ideas are fantastic. We've been discussing revisions to many of the Peterson holdings. Blake will be back sometime next week, and I'm sure he'd love to know you're open to adjusting your whimsical nostalgic plan. Maybe even letting go of it. I mean, your plans are cute and all, but Blake's vision for the place is so much better. It would be so much easier for all of us concerned if you agree." There was nothing friendly in the woman's smile.

"You've seen the plans? And discussed all this with Blake?" Zoe asked, unable to keep the surprise from her voice.

"Of course. Blake darling shares everything with me, and we talk all the time. I can't wait until he gets home. My daddy has got a welcome party planned for him. Oops, maybe I shouldn't have mentioned the party. Forgive me. I can't invite you as it's really only for our closest friends and family. Blake and I have a big announcement to make."

Lindsey approached, setting a soda down in front of Zoe. "Here you go, boss," Lindsay said, the frown on her face a good indicator she'd overheard Tammy's comments and had strong feelings on the subject matter.

Feelings that echoed Zoe's. It was so much worse than anything she could have expected. Not in her wildest dreams would she have thought Blake—the anti-relationship guy, would be getting married. And to Tammy. Zoe glanced at her left hand, still not wanting to believe the woman. "Thank you," she said softly, Lindsey moving off to help another customer.

"We aren't engaged—yet." Tammy kept talking as if anyone listening would be hanging on the edge of their seats for whatever she had to say. But it was Tammy's conspiratorial grin that made Zoe want to throw up.

"I see. I guess congratulations will soon be in order. I hope the two of you will be quite happy." Not that she expected it to happen, but Zoe wouldn't give the woman the satisfaction of an undignified outburst. Showing anything other than indifference would make her look like a love-sick fool. "As to the renovation for the creamery, whatever Blake wants, he can do. He is the boss, after all." Zoe found it hard to breathe, whether from Tammy's perfume or her news, or both, she had to get away.

"Thank you, that's very kind. I'm sure he'll appreciate your cooperation. He's such a handsome man, I'll be sure to keep a close eye on him if you know what I mean." Tammy's gaze narrowed slightly.

Enough was enough. Zoe stood. "If you're into that sort of thing. Computer geek, city boy. More metro than my tastes."

Tammy nodded. "I know what you mean. That's why I dumped him in high school, but I realize the error of my ways. I see beneath his exterior and know his heart. And I know we will be quite happy together." The syrupy sweet words dripped from Tammy's ruby-red lips like icicles.

Lindsey approached. "Here you—" The sundae slipped out of her hands, landing on Tammy's lap, chocolate fudge coloring the pink wool of her slacks as she jumped to her feet in horror.

"How dare you!" Tammy exclaimed, grabbing several napkins to brush the ice cream and sauce off, making a bigger mess in the process.

"I'm sorry," Lindsey said. "Let me get you more napkins and a wet cloth."

"Don't come near me. You've done enough. Wait until I talk to Blake about this. I'll have you fired, you bumbling fool." Tammy's rage had caused her face to flush a splotchy pink that matched her slacks.

"I'm sure she didn't mean it," Zoe said, trying to clean up some of the mess as Teddy came over with a mop and bucket of water. "Maybe if you went into the restroom, it would be easier to clean up the worst of it," she suggested.

"I'll do nothing of the sort. These are dry clean only," she huffed. "I've got to get back to work, but I'm so glad we got to have this little chat. Other than the part where your inept server dumped ice cream on me, that is."

"I do apologize, and yes, I'm glad we had this little chat," Zoe said, the words almost choking her as she uttered them. The last thing she wanted to do was apologize. She made her way behind the counter as Tammy strode out of the creamery.

Zoe looked at Lindsey, the girl's unabashed twinkling in her eyes giving way to something she hadn't considered. "If you dumped it on her lap on purpose, I wouldn't write you up."

Lindsay's surprised expression brought her great satisfaction. It was wrong, and Zoe shouldn't have said it, but the words slipped out, her frustration at an all-time high.

"Seriously?" the girl asked.

"No. I was but teasing." Zoe tried to backstroke a bit. "You didn't, did you?"

"Oh, no, boss lady. Although I must say, she's genuinely not a nice person. But I guess it doesn't matter as it would seem she didn't want the sundae after all." Lindsey fought back a grin as she denied any willful wrongdoing.

"Good, glad to hear it," Zoe said, shooting the girl a wink before she headed toward the back room. The ice cream sundae dump couldn't have happened to a nicer person.

In her office, Zoe sat down, resting her elbows on the desk as she cradled her chin. She let out a deep breath. This was a disaster. She'd wanted confirmation from Blake about his relationship with Tammy, but the woman's admission required no further details or explanation. *Getting married said it all.*

This would never work. Before she lost her nerve, Zoe sat down and typed out an email. More specifically, a resignation letter.

The money would tide them over while she found a new job, and her title as manager should open a few doors. Unfortunately, the dream vacation wasn't a reality any longer. Scott would be devastated, but there was no way Zoe could stand by and watch Blake renovate the shop his way, destroying the history of the place. And worse, stand by and watch him and Tammy parade around as an engaged couple.

Chapter Twenty-One

♥

BLAKE STILL COULDN'T BELIEVE Zoe had up and quit, not even bothering to discuss the decision with him. He knew she was upset the night of the party but quitting her job was over the top. He'd gotten the news right before he was finished packing and getting his apartment on the market. At one point, he'd thought about keeping the place, but the idea of going all-in had merit. He wanted to give it his best shot to make the position of CTO work and that meant not having a place to bounce back to.

Including his job at Modern Design Tech. They hadn't been pleased he was leaving but were more on board once he agreed to finish handling the projects he'd already been working on. And he'd agreed to take on a few projects as a consultant going forward.

It was a win-win situation for him, just like the one he'd arranged with Wade Wright. The man loved his ideas for the creamery and wanted Blake to work on a few designs for his private company, the one he owned and operated outside of the law firm. Blake had been only too willing to agree, knowing it would be a great way to keep him busy as he worked through the changes at Peterson's. And even more importantly, keep him busy after everything was up and running. The only downside had been Tammy's involvement in the whole matter, her presence becoming more and more irritating with each passing day.

Blake quickly set Wade straight about his intentions toward Tammy, and from that point forward, the two men worked well together. Lucky for him, the man wasn't one to let anything get in the way of good business. Not even his daughter, no matter how much he doted on her.

His friendship with Zoe had bolstered his own confidence levels, and it was no longer an exterior show. *What you see is what you get* was his new motto in life. And it was more proof they would have been good together, except she'd made her point loud and clear. She wanted nothing to do with him.

And without Zoe in the picture, Blake saw no reason not to put his own plans for the creamery into action. It took him less than a week to close the shop and have contractors showing up. Of course, he was using most of the ones Zoe had already hired. To them, it didn't matter which plan they followed, as long as they got paid.

It felt good to be a part of the hands-on action instead of designing and then handing his drawings over to others to implement. It also paid off to have a lot of contacts willing to expedite the process. The only problem was that the further they got into the renovation, the less satisfied Blake was with the project.

There was something missing, and it didn't take him long to figure it out. It was unfortunate he'd wasted a week already, but he could finally admit the truth.

Zoe had been right all along.

Peterson's Ice Creamery had history, and without it, the place lost its individuality. On top of that, he realized the place also didn't feel right because of Zoe's absence. The way he saw it, he had a huge problem—and it was up to him to fix it.

Zoe was as much a part of the creamery as she was in his life. *He'd fallen in love.*

The reason he never dated a woman longer than a couple of weeks was because he was dating the wrong kind of women. That's why Tammy had irritated him like a splinter whenever she was around. She was like all the others he'd dated, and she wasn't Zoe.

Could never be Zoe.

"Hey, everyone. Let's call it quits for the day. I've got to talk to my grandfather about something before we go any further," Blake announced to all the contractors in the creamery.

Everyone stopped what they were doing. Saws, drills, and hammers fell silent. The workers seemed unsure what to make of his comment.

"Whatever you want, you're the boss." Greg Miller, the foreman, was the first to recover. The others nodded in agreement and started to gather their belongings. Who wouldn't want an early out day? In less than ten minutes, the place had cleared out.

Twenty minutes after that, he found his grandfather alone at the house, which suited Blake's purpose just fine. The last thing he wanted at the moment was to deal with his father's negativity or his *I-told-you-so* comments.

"Hey, Grandpa. Was there any extra of that casserole?" Sarah had made a macaroni and tomato dish that was as good as the one their mother used to make, and another helping would satisfy the rumbling in his stomach.

"Sure, still plenty in the fridge. What are you doing home?" he asked, watching Blake as he crossed the kitchen.

He pulled a plate down from the cupboard just as Hank came charging in the room, bouncing around, tail wagging, excited at the prospect of a meal or an outdoor run. Neither of which he'd be getting just yet. He patted the dog on the head. "No, Hank. Lay down. I'll take you out later," he said, giving him a treat for behaving so well. Blake looked up at his grandfather. "I wanted to talk to you about something if you've got a few minutes."

His grandfather nodded. "I've always got time for you. Heat up your plate and come sit down."

Blake took out the casserole, ladled a helping onto his plate, and placed it in the microwave. After setting the timer and pressing start, he put the rest of the macaroni and tomatoes back in the refrigerator and waited, trying to formulate his thoughts. The timer dinged, and he grabbed a potholder to remove the plate, joining his grandfather at the table.

"So, what's eating at you? Your brain is churning ninety miles an hour," he said, a frown on his wrinkled face. His grandfather knew him inside and out, better than anyone, in fact.

Blake let out a huge sigh. Admitting you were wrong didn't come easy, and this was about so much more than a simple mistake. It was time for the truth. "The creamery. The renovation. Zoe. Everything."

His grandfather pushed his plate away and sat back. "I'll need more than that, Blake."

"It started with Zoe leaving. I thought with her gone, it was a smooth path to do the remodeling more in line with what I'd imagined, thinking entirely of the bottom-line profits. But everything I'm doing feels flat. It looked great on paper, but the reality, not so much. I feel like my first project as CTO is a bust." Failure was a miserable friend, and he prided himself on getting things done right. So why when it was his most important mission, had he let that pride get in the way?

"Then fix it. I'm not going to fire you," the old man said, grinning. "Profits aren't everything. People matter. The creamery has heart, and you can't take the heart out of the place."

If his grandfather felt this way, the time for the lecture would have been before he started changing up the plans. Then it would have been an avoidable disaster. "Why didn't you stop me?"

His grandfather shrugged. "That's easy—it was your decision, and I wasn't going to get in the way, no matter whether I wanted to or not." It was mind-boggling to realize he'd let Blake fail on purpose.

Fix it. He would try, but some things he felt might be beyond repair. "Why did you vote for Zoe? I know why Dad did, but I was surprised when I found out about you." It was a question that had burned in his heart since Zoe had been announced the winner.

"I voted for Zoe because I liked her designs. They touched me and brought back memories. She's got good instincts."

"I thought you called me home to see what progress could do for Peterson's, and that you were on board with moving the company into the future. I thought that's why you'd want high tech in the creamery. Was this some sort of game to you?"

"Hardly. You're right, I did call you home to see what you could do for the company. Do I need to point out that you're still here?" He smiled, running a hand through his thinning gray hair. "The reason for the contest was because I also believe in Zoe, and she didn't believe in herself. I needed to push her outside her comfort zone and take charge, not wait for life to happen. I didn't expect her to quit and was quite upset when she did. I tried to talk her out of it, but she turned on a stubborn streak I hadn't witnessed before. Seems my plan backfired."

This was all news to Blake. The contest had been for Zoe's sake? No wonder his grandfather voted for her. It was his plan for her to win all along and manage the shop. *Something Zoe had earned.* It made sense that his grandfather knew all this, but he was also right about the plan backfiring in a way he hadn't counted on.

"At least she talked to you. She hasn't spoken to me at all."

"Have you bothered to call her?" he asked.

Blake shook his head. "No. I think she's made her position clear. My focus is on the creamery, and now, more than ever, I need to switch gears and find a way to redo the place with a little more of a nostalgic touch. That's a tall order, but at least I know you'll approve."

"I'm glad to see you making the right choice for the creamery. But I'd hate to see you make a wrong one about Zoe. You know, she's a lot like your grandmother was at that age. Headstrong and impulsive. She was a good person, a better woman, and the best wife."

Blake was more than a little surprised at his grandfather's admission. Unfortunately, it was too late. He was in love with Zoe, of that he was sure, but a one-sided relationship wasn't what he had in mind. "Well, you know me. I'm not the marrying kind of guy."

"People change," his grandfather said, with a nod of his head. "I heard she canceled the trip to Disney. Such a shame. I know Scott was looking forward to it. I did tell her I'd give her a good recommendation any place she applied to work. It was the least I could do after all the years she dedicated to the creamery. "Except now, his grandfather's recommendation included a more personalized approach.

A matchmaking one.

"I hadn't heard that. I hate it for them, as it seems to me they both deserved a break. Poor kid was so excited when she told him."

"Reckon there's something you could do about that," his grandfather said, a wide grin on his face. The old coot wasn't letting up on getting him and Zoe together. And the more Blake thought about it, the better the idea sounded.

Now all he had to do was convince Zoe, and he had a feeling the renovation of the creamery could be his golden ticket. "Can I have her contest proposal? think maybe I should do the place over exactly as she planned." Not to mention, Team Zoe still worked at the creamery and would be all too willing to pitch in and help him.

His grandfather grinned. "Best idea you've had yet. I think you're going to make an excellent CTO."

Blake stood, taking his plate to the sink. "Let's hope you're right. *And* that we can get her to come to the grand opening."

"I like the way you're thinking. You should talk to your sister. She's pretty good with creative ideas, trust me." His grandfather chuckled, winking at Blake as he stood. "I'll be right back with the plans," he said, handing Blake his plate.

His grandfather was right again. If anyone could get Zoe to come to the grand opening, it would be Sarah.

Chapter Twenty-Two

♥

IT HAD BEEN ALMOST three weeks, and with each day that passed, Zoe still found herself thinking about Blake. He hadn't called, and she avoided the creamery and any other place she might run into him. After the first week, she'd seen Chad at the post office and he'd been quick to tell her about Blake replacing her ideas for the renovation with his own high-tech designs. It broke her heart to even think of the destruction of the landmark business that represented the very essence of Hallbrook and small-town living.

The job search had yet to pan out into anything solid, but she did have a second interview today at the Le Croissant bakery in Lancaster. A manager's position no less, and right up her alley—except, Zoe wasn't all that excited about it. Her heart hadn't been into job hunting when she started looking, and nothing had changed.

For Scott either. He still took every opportunity to complain about her deviation from the plans, unwilling to give up the vacation without resistance. Maybe if the job in Lancaster came through, in a year when she'd be eligible for vacations, she'd make a point of taking him. It was the best she could offer at this point, but patience wasn't Scott's virtue.

Zoe walked the short distance from the nearby town center parking lot to the bakery. She adjusted her hat and smoothed out her hair, trying to look presentable. Steve Dillion spotted her and walked in her direction, a friendly smile on his face.

He reached out to shake her hand. "Thanks for coming back today. We were really impressed with your qualifications, and I wanted to discuss the management position with you further." Mr. Dillion held the door open for her to enter.

"Sounds good to me," she said, following him to the back offices.

"Can I get you anything? A coffee and a donut, perhaps?" Super friendly and thoughtful were good characteristics for a boss to have.

Zoe removed her coat and hung it on the rack. "No, thanks. I've got to pick up my son at three today, so I can't linger. I want to make sure I have time to answer any remaining questions you may have, and then I've got a few questions of my own." She settled into the chair in front of his oversized desk, crossing her legs, and trying to portray a confident and in-control look.

"I like it. Let's get to it then, shall we?" Mr. Dillion opened the file in front of him. "One of my biggest concerns is your lack of time as a manager at Peterson's. What happened that you left them so quickly after your promotion?"

"It's a fair question, and one I've asked myself quite often. For a long time, I was doing most of the responsibilities associated with what the manager's position entailed, but the promotion just never seemed to come up. I guess I didn't ask, and they didn't offer. In reality, I've been managing the place for years. Peterson's Human Resources department always handled the employee hiring process, reviews, and raises." Honesty was best because for the life of her, nothing else would even sound remotely plausible. Not to mention, it had been drilled into her by her parents and in church. Lies only complicated the truth, it never made it better.

Mr. Dillion nodded, glancing down at her resume. "What changed after they gave you the title? After only a week if I'm reading this correctly." He pointed at the entry referencing her dates of employment. "Do you mind elaborating on that a bit?"

Zoe let out a deep breath. "It was personal. Mr. Peterson hired his grandson as the new Chief of Technology, and he and I weren't on good terms. It would have made for a difficult working relationship, and I felt it best to move on. There was no sense continuing to fight an uphill battle. We simply didn't see eye to eye on a lot of things." All true. Yet still heartbreaking.

"I see. Well, their loss is our gain." He smiled. "Do you see your son's schedule to be an issue since you're, umm, a single parent?" Mr. Dillion's smile had disappeared, the man was clearly uncomfortable with the question. *As he should be*. He didn't have the right to ask, but seeing as it didn't matter, and she needed a job, there was no sense in calling him out over it

"No. My son goes to a friend's house after school. It's only with me currently home that I've taken advantage and made it so I'm spending more time with Scott."

"That's good. I'm sure you're a wonderful mother, and your son is a lucky boy. So, what questions did you have for me?" Mr. Dillion sat back in his leather chair, the springs squeaking.

"Questions about pay scale, vacations, holidays—that sort of thing," she said. All stuff that hadn't come up in the first interview and they were important to her.

Mr. Dillion nodded. "Of course." He slid open one of the desk drawers and pulled out a manual, flipping it to one of the color-coded sections. "This is what we offer." He turned the book toward her and began listing off the bullet points one by one. No personalization whatsoever.

"Thank you. These seem to all be standard policies. And what about the pay scale?" she asked, knowing it was the most important question. She never understood why potential employers wouldn't bring it up earlier in the interview process. If the money wasn't right, the rest of the conversation was a moot point and a waste of both their times.

"The job would pay a salary of thirty-three thousand dollars annually, paid biweekly. We'd like to offer more, but we're a small shop." He looked somewhat embarrassed as he named off the number.

What he didn't know was that it was more than she'd been making at the creamery. Not by much, but still more and, therefore, acceptable. She wasn't going backward if she could help it. "The salary would be fine," she said, trying to put him at ease.

"Well, is there anything else you want to know?" he asked, looking relieved.

Zoe shook her head. "Not that I can think of."

"Well, in that case, we'd like to offer you the position with a start date of a week from next Monday if you're interested. With you not working, I can imagine you're eager to get back to work, but the person designated to train you is currently on vacation." Something Zoe still hadn't managed to do for her and Scott. It was a bright spot on the horizon and something to look forward to.

"I am, and thank you." The problem was, she still wasn't sure this was what she wanted to do. "Can I let you know for sure in a day or so? I feel as though it would be better to move to Lancaster if I were going to accept the position, especially with the treacherous conditions of the winter roads between here and Hallbrook. It's a big decision, especially since I would have to move Scott to a new school." Changes in life always came with complications, this one more than its fair share. She couldn't believe she was risking losing out on the job, but time to think it over knowing all the details was important to her.

"That's fine. Take all the time you need. We'd love to have you work with us, but we pride ourselves on having happy employees." Mr. Dillion stood, a warm and sincere smile on his face.

"Thanks, Mr. Dillion." She reached out to shake his hand.

"Call me Steve," he said, responding with a hearty handshake.

"Well, then, thanks, Steve." Zoe turned to leave.

"No problem. I look forward to hearing from you with an answer."

Zoe was out of her mind. She should have accepted right there and then. The money was good, the benefits were good, the owner of the shop was great. What else was it she wanted?

Peterson's.

And Blake.

Two things she couldn't have.

Zoe got in her car and headed for home. Her phone rang, the sound muffled as it came from inside her purse. She dug through the oversized bag with one hand, keeping her eyes on the road. "Hey, Sarah. What's up? I haven't heard from you in a bit."

"I could say the same of you. Just because you quit working at the shop doesn't mean we can't be friends. Or hang out."

Sarah was right, but between the added pressure of looking for a job and Scott's attitude issues, she hadn't wanted to burden her friend. Not to mention, it did feel slightly awkward. "You know that's not it at all. I've been busy with job hunting."

"How's the job search coming, anyway?"

"Great. Actually, I just got an employment offer. The only problem is it would be smarter for me to move to Lancaster if I take it." It wasn't the only problem, but it was certainly one of them. It would have the added benefit of ensuring she wouldn't run into Blake and Tammy. That was a definite positive.

"Move?" Sarah squeaked out. "Are you serious? Where is this job, Boston?"

"Lancaster." It sounded lame when now that she'd said it.

"Oh, for Pete's sake, commute like everyone else does." And Sarah knew it. Her friend wouldn't give in easy on this one.

"Not everyone has an older car and a son to take care of. It's important that I can get to work and get him to school on time and picked up after." She wasn't sure who she was trying to convince, Sarah or herself.

"You can't move. It's out of the question. Who will go to O'Malley's with me on Friday nights? Tell me you haven't accepted." Her friend was grasping at straws. And she was using the same argument twice—on opposite sides. It was okay to commute for work, but not to O'Malley's.

Zoe appreciated that her friend cared, and she felt a whole lot better. About everything. Life wasn't turning out the way Zoe wanted, but her one constant was Sarah. Life was always better with a best friend. "Not yet, but I can't think of a good reason not to."

"Other than you'd be leaving your best friend behind."

"Stop with the attempt to guilt me into staying. Thirty minutes isn't leaving you behind." Zoe laughed.

"Whatever. You can't accept it. At least not until you do something fun with me," Sarah insisted.

Her friend's persistence left Zoe to wonder what she was up to. "Like what?"

"Come to the grand reopening of Peterson's. For me."

Zoe let out a deep breath. Sarah was asking her to do the one thing she wouldn't do. "Sarah, you know I can't. It would be awkward." Worse than awkward, but Sarah didn't know the half of it.

"Awkward for who? Everyone there misses you. Big deal, you quit. But that doesn't mean you can't ever have ice cream again. We're not six, you know." Sarah laughed.

"Don't exaggerate. I'm sure not everyone misses me." Blake most assuredly hadn't given her a second thought.

"I'm not asking you to do this for Blake; do it for me."

"Who said anything about Blake?" she said, trying to misdirect the conversation.

"Look, I know you two have had your differences, but it's time to move forward. Last time I checked, you won the contest. Not to mention, you have a new job offer. Your confidence level has to be pretty high right about now. I think you should embrace that confidence and show up. Show them you don't care and that you've moved on. It's important to me." Sarah had a flair for the dramatic, but she was right on several points.

"I don't know what to say. You are laying it on a bit too thick, although I will give in and admit having a job offer on the table makes it better." Zoe couldn't believe she was thinking about agreeing to her friend's request.

"Say yes. Please," Sarah pressed for her acceptance, not letting up until she got her way.

Zoe turned into the Parker's driveway and shut
off the car. "Yes."

"You mean it? You'll come? And you should bring
Scott. It'll be so much fun." Sarah laughed.

Might as well go all the way at this point. "Okay,
and yes, I'll bring Scott. Maybe it will get me off his
bad list. When is it?" Zoe asked.

"Saturday. One p.m. sharp."

Zoe gripped the steering wheel, an eerie sensa-
tion coming over her. Sarah was up to something.
Perhaps she should have trusted her initial instinct
and said no. "Why sharp? It's an informal event,
isn't it?"

"Sort of. Gemma Duncan is hosting the event and
her parties are fabulous," Sarah said as if that in
itself was a reasonable explanation.

It wasn't too late to change her mind, but she
wouldn't. The old Zoe might have turned tail and
run, but Sarah was right—whatever happened, Zoe
would deal with it. Life was throwing her curves,
but the difference now was she was swinging the
bat. Hopefully, she didn't strikeout. "That does

sound like fun. I really like her. Remember the rescue squad fundraiser last year? Now that was incredible. Never seen anything like it, and she put it together in record time."

"She was on point and in love. Love creates miracles in people's lives."

"Not everyone's," Zoe quipped. Her friend's love and happiness with Dalton was bubbling over into her entire life.

"That remains to be seen," Sarah said, not backing down. "I've got to run. See you there. Oh, and Zoe, one other thing," she said hesitantly.

"What's that?"

"Promise me you won't accept the new job offer until after Saturday." Sarah's request took Zoe by surprise. The two weren't connected, so why would it matter?

"I shouldn't keep Steve hanging. I wouldn't want him to change his mind." Zoe laughed.

"Steve?" Sarah asked, her voice suddenly serious.

"The owner."

"Promise?" she insisted. There was a determined edge in her voice, one Zoe recognized. Sarah wouldn't give up on this until she agreed.

"Fine. I promise. You drive a hard bargain, but it can't hurt to wait, and he did say to take my time."

"See you then. Thanks, Zoe. I've got to run." The excitement in Sarah's voice was undeniably back, leaving Zoe to wonder again exactly what her friend was up to.

Chapter Twenty-Three

♥

A LARGE CROWD HAD gathered outside the ice cream shop on Saturday, and Zoe was having a tough time spotting Sarah. "Do you see her, Scott?"

"Nope. Lots of people want ice cream. It'll take forever to get some," Scott said, a pouty smile on his face.

His mood had brightened considerably when she mentioned taking him for ice cream today, but his good mood only went so far. "It'll be fine, trust me. Grand openings are always busy, and I promised Sarah we'd meet up for it. I'm sure they have everyone working, so it'll go super-fast. At least it's not cold anymore." Pointing out the positives was always a good thing.

"Look, Mom. There she is," he shouted, pointing toward the far back of the crowd on the opposite side of where they stood.

Sarah waved, spotting them at the same time. Her friend's bright smile was filled with excitement as she made her way toward them. "Boy, am I ever glad to see you."

"I did promise, and a promise is a promise. There are a ton of people here. Couldn't we do this later?"

"And miss out on all the fun? No way." Sarah waved at a few people, and Zoe relaxed, doing the same, responding to friendly hellos and the cheery attitudes of all those gathered for the big event.

Brown paper covered the window, keeping the inside a secret. The old sign had been left in place, which Zoe considered odd, but perhaps Blake hadn't had time to change it yet. She couldn't picture a neon flashing sign for Peterson's. Not one bit.

Sharply at one, the doors to the creamery were opened. Blake and his grandfather stepped outside, both dressed casually in jeans and sweaters. The two were of the same height and similar build, something Zoe hadn't noticed before.

Blake raised his arm in the air and waved. "Good afternoon, everyone. Can I have your attention for just a minute?"

The crowd fell silent.

"I'd like to welcome you all to the new and improved version of Peterson's Ice Creamery. The shop has been around for almost fifty years and was in much need of updating. I hope you'll agree the new look is better and more entertaining, and of course, encourages you to visit more often." Everyone chuckled.

Blake scanned the crowd, his gaze landing on her. His smile grew wider, and with it, the tension she was feeling evaporated. "I know everyone is eager to come inside, but I do have one special request. Can you all help me out and make room for one very special guest here today?"

Everyone looked around, nodding in agreement, their whispering murmurs growing louder as they wondered who he was talking about. Zoe already knew. *His fiancée.*

Surely Sarah hadn't dragged her here to witness the announcement. That would be heartless, not something she identified with her friend. Whatever tension had dissipated was now like a twenty-pound weight in her gut. She shouldn't have come. Wiping at her eyes, she brushed back the tears welling there. Zoe gripped Scott's hand harder, causing him to look up at her. She shook her head and shrugged, not knowing what to say. It was nothing she could explain to a nine-year-old.

The crowd parted, reminding her of the Bible story of when Moses parted the Dead Sea, everyone looking around, still wondering who it would be.

"Zoe Carruthers, can you make your way forward to the front?" Blake said.

Wait. What?

She hadn't misheard him. Everyone was looking at her, urging her forward. She pulled Scott with her, shooting Sarah a dirty look first. The wide grin on her face a clear indicator she'd known all about this, the brat. Zoe had been set up—for what, she didn't have a clue.

"Good to see you, Zoe," Blake smiled warmly before taking her hand and guiding her up the step. "Hey, Scott, good to see you again, buddy."

Her son's happy-go-lucky expression had returned. Blake had singled them out and he was in his element. Probably because he was moving to the front of the line for ice cream. But, admittedly, also because it was Blake.

"It's good to see you both," Zoe said, shaking hands with Mack Peterson first. She would put on a good front. The new Zoe could handle this. And it wasn't like she'd been given a choice. Sarah would have a lot of explaining to do after.

"Hi, Zoe. Glad you could make it today. You're in for a real treat," Mr. Peterson said, surprising her. She'd thought Old Man Peterson was all for preserving the history of the creamery, so his comment made no sense. Much the same as his presence here, looking as if he were pleased with the outcome. Proud of his grandson.

"Thanks. It's not like I had a choice with Sarah pressuring me. I just don't understand why I'm here and what this is about," Zoe responded, voicing the question utmost in her mind.

"We were counting on her." The old man winked. "As to why you're here front and center, I'll let you be the judge in a few moments." His eyes twinkled with merriment as he laughed.

"Thanks for coming, Zoe," Blake said, reaching out to take her hand. "It means a lot to me."

"Like I said, Sarah left me little choice. So what's going on?"

"Hang on, and I'll show you. It's way better than telling." He chuckled. Blake still hadn't released her hand as he turned to address the crowd once more.

"My grandfather, the founder of Peterson's, will soon let you all in. He's going to hand out numbers, and you'll be called to the register to place your order. This will give you time to look around the shop and keep everything orderly. I hope you all enjoy the new Peterson's."

Clapping broke out, signaling their approval of the plan.

Blake pulled Zoe forward. "Shall we?"

"Sure, why not." Zoe couldn't help but wonder where Tammy was, the woman not likely to miss such an important event or the limelight. More than likely, controlling the staff inside to make sure everything was done to perfection. That would certainly be her style.

They stepped inside and stopped. Zoe couldn't believe her eyes. Everything she'd planned out in her designs, right down to the last detail, had been added. She glanced at Blake. "I don't understand. I thought—"

"You thought wrong. Well, you were right at first, but then something happened, and I changed my mind."

She glanced around the shop, thrilled to see the pinball machines, soda fountains, red-leather stools, checkered tablecloths, candy jars overflowing with beautiful colors to tempt customers, and so much more. "What happened?" she asked, turning back to him.

"You did." Blake wasn't making any sense.

He led her around the shop, pointing out some of the not so obvious details. All from her designs.

"Wow, this is way cool. Isn't it, Mom?" Scott asked, his eyes filled with excitement.

"Ummm, yes, it is." It was better than way cool; it was a dream come true.

"That's because your mother designed it," Blake told Scott.

"She did?" Her son looked up at her for confirmation, a confused expression on his face. "But you don't work here anymore."

"I don't. But remember the contest I won? This was the design proposal I submitted. It would seem Blake used it to renovate." She still couldn't believe her eyes. And Sarah hadn't let on one bit, the stinker.

"Of course, I remember. It's when I was promised a trip to Disney that never happened." His face scrunched up at the memory.

"Go easy on your mom. She has a lot to deal with, and I'm sure she thought her decision to leave Peterson's was the right one. Grown-up stuff isn't always easy to understand, but you should trust she was making the best decision for both of you at the time." Blake defending her life choices came as another shock. But if he was okay with her leaving, it also meant he hadn't missed her. She was sure Tammy and the renovations were occupying all of his time.

"Thank you, Blake. He's been sore with me since I left the company. You've done an amazing job." Her heart swelled with the emotion of seeing her designs come to life. It was just as she'd imagined. Or better. It was real. Just like the man next to her. She closed her eyes, trying to fight back the reality of her love, knowing Blake was out of reach. Figuratively, not literally.

Literally, he still held her hand.

"We'll see what we can do to fix things. Okay, buddy?"

Scott's instant smile was back in place. "I like the sound of that. Did you hear that, Mom? Blake is going to fix things."

Zoe shook her head, some of the excitement of the moment fading. "Blake, don't. It's been hard enough as it is, and it's just not possible. I'm starting a new job at Le Croissant in Lancaster, and vacation time isn't earned until after you complete your first year. Kids aren't known for patience."

"Sarah said you hadn't accepted yet. You haven't, right?" Blake asked, concern written in his expression.

Zoe shrugged, tilting her head to one side. "Well, no. Not formally anyway. But I'm planning on it come Monday morning, and I start the following week."

"Don't." One single word that held a depth of meaning Zoe couldn't even begin to understand.

"Don't what?" she asked. "Take the job? I have to work. It's not really an option."

"You don't have to take it. Look around you, Zoe. The creamery has your rubber stamp of approval on every inch of it. I did this for you, hoping you'll come back to Peterson's. You've been a part of this place a long time. In a way, you're a part of its history, and the place wouldn't be the same without you in it." Coming from Blake, the words were high praise, his offer to come back to Peterson's warming her heart. Unfortunately, it wouldn't change her answer.

"That's a very kind thing to say, but I simply can't come back. My reasons for leaving had nothing to do with the changes I thought you would make. Or, well, at least they were only part of the reason." The new and more confidant Zoe would tell Blake the truth and walk away. And after he'd done all this to get her to come back, it was the least she could do. It was time to take charge of her life, and that included her feelings for Blake. "Scott, why don't you go order, honey? Get me a Maple Walnut cone, please. And tell them I'll pay before I leave."

"Ice cream is a nickel a scoop today. I even rolled back the prices to opening day in 1953." He reached in his pocket and pulled out some money. "Here, take this to pay for the ice cream, and leave this in the tip jar." He handed Scott a five-dollar bill.

"Gee, thanks, Blake." Scott was gone in a flash.

"What's really going on, Zoe? I had hoped you would love this enough to come back."

She let out a deep breath. "It's you. I can't work with you." There, she'd said it. It didn't make her feel one iota better. There was nothing freeing about this moment.

He dropped her hand, a pained expression on his face. "You hate me that much? Why? I thought we got along quite well, especially when we were working together. This doesn't make any sense. You've avoided me ever since the promotion was announced. Surely, you're not threatened by my title or the fact I'd be your boss. That's not like you at all."

Zoe looked away, her gaze landing on her son. She let out another deep breath. "The boss thing is a part of it, or it was before. I was worried you'd change the design since you had the power to do so.

I didn't want to see the place change, preferring to keep my own memories."

"I wouldn't have interfered with what you wanted. You won fair and square. It was only after you left that I decided to change the plans. But after I started on them, they just weren't working. The further I got into the renovation, the more I realized the truth. That's when I switched gears, got your proposal from my grandfather, and went gung-ho to do everything the way you wanted. Like I said, part of the motive was to bring you back. You belong here, Zoe." There was a desperation in his voice that hadn't been there before. And everything he said hit home, making her want to come back.

No. Tammy still existed, and she couldn't bear to watch them together. Their last meeting flashed before her, the woman staking a claim on her man and her future power to control everything. It was the same meeting Tammy mentioned she and Blake had gone over Zoe's designs and discussed them. "Wait a minute. Did you say you got the proposal from your grandfather after you'd already started on your plans?"

"Yes. Why?" He frowned.

Something wasn't adding up. "Tammy mentioned you'd shown the designs to her before I ever left Peterson's."

"Tammy? What's she got to do with this?" Blake's surprise was genuine.

"She stopped by the creamery and we had a chat." There was only one way to find out the truth. Something she should have done before. "About everything. I guess congratulations are in order," Zoe said, watching him closely for his reaction.

"Congratulations for what? Reopening the shop?" The lines across his forehead and his confusion were real, his reaction not a disappointment. And if the shop was his first thought, what about the rest?

"Men. Always thinking business first. I meant on your engagement," Zoe exclaimed.

"Why would you think I'm engaged?" Blake's expression changed to one of shock, immediately followed by one of scorn. "Let me guess—Tammy."

"Well, yes. She said—"

Blake shook his head. "I don't care what she said. Most of what comes out of her mouth are lies. It was the same way back in high school, and it's still very much that way." So, they weren't engaged—or even getting engaged by the sounds of it.

"I don't understand. You two went to dinner, and I heard..." Zoe clapped a hand over her mouth.

"You heard wrong. I had a dinner meeting with her father, and she showed up to tell me he was delayed—and she stayed through dinner. Not of my choosing. It was a business meeting," Blake said, his tone very matter of fact.

"Business?" she squeaked.

"Yes. He's hired me to do some contract designs for him. And I accepted, but only after I set the record straight that his daughter wasn't part of the deal."

"So, you're not—

"A couple. Hardly. I'm in love with someone else," Blake said, a smile returning to his face.

"You are?" she asked, dumbfounded by his comment. "I thought you said you didn't believe in relationships." Zoe racked her brain, trying to figure out who the lucky woman could be.

"I don't. Or I didn't. Turns out I was dating the wrong kind of women. I've discovered my tastes run slightly more country." Blake chuckled.

Zoe had to ask, not coming up with anyone as a candidate—unless... "So, who are you dating?"

Blake grinned. "No one, at least not yet."

Zoe's heart pounded in her chest. She didn't dare let herself hope, but it would seem hope was blossoming out of control. "But you're in love. You're not making any sense, Blake."

He reached for her hand and pulled her close. "We never officially dated, but I'm seriously in love—with you."

Her eyes grew wide, her heart racing in overtime. Blake Peterson just said he loved her, or at least she thought he did. "With me?" she squeaked out, just to be sure.

"Yes, you. Zoe, I want you back at Peterson's, but I also want you back in my life, with me. I love you." Blake leaned forward, dropping a kiss on her lips. "Say something, sweetheart."

"Oh," she said, still dumbfounded, her brain not catching up with her heart.

"I'd hoped for a little more than that. Maybe a confession you feel the same?" he asked, grinning.

"I do," she said in a breathless whisper, going up on tiptoe to kiss Blake, showing him with words and action how much she cared.

The sounds of clapping interrupted the kiss.

They stepped apart, but Blake didn't let her go. "Please put me out of my misery and tell me you'll come back."

"Yes, I'll come back." Zoe smiled, the joy in her heart overflowing.

"To the shop, me, or both?" he asked, keeping her close.

"Both. The reason I left was that I'd fallen in love with you, and I couldn't bear to see you with—"

"Don't say it. Never put her name and mine in the same sentence. You are the only woman for me. Forever and ever," Blake said, the love shining in his eyes directed at her.

"It's about time you two figured out what I've known for over ten years," Sarah said, joining them. "Nice kiss, by the way. Even better than the one at the birthday party."

Blake shook his head. "You've got it all wrong. I've only just figured out—"

"Hogwash. You used to watch her as much as she used to watch you. The thought of you two together in high school freaked me out. I was afraid you'd steal my best friend, brother dear. Now, the thought of you two not together is concerning. Especially after your wholehearted agreement to stay away from her. It was a bit over-the-top of a reaction, which is when I knew you still cared about her. I want Zoe as my sister, and it's clear you two belong together."

Blake and Zoe smiled at each other, silly, loving smiles.

"I'll see what I can do to arrange that," Blake said, his comment sending a fresh wave of delight down her spine.

"Let's hope you're as good at arranging as I am," Sarah said, the smirk on her face irresistible.

"What did you do?" Zoe asked, casting a frown in her friend's direction.

"After the famous birthday kiss the entire town was talking about, I figured I had to do something to make sure you figured out what everyone else already knew. Let's see, the contest for one. Blake's date being canceled for seconds. And thirdly, getting you here today. I'm good like that," Sarah said, not an ounce of regret or guilt in her voice.

"I heard about the contest from Grandpa, and I know about you getting Zoe here, but what's this about my date being canceled?" Blake asked.

Sarah's smile only grew bigger. "I took auto shop, dodo head. I pulled your starter plug so you couldn't go. I didn't want you sidetracked while I was trying to figure out how to get you both to see what was right in front of your face."

"You little minx. I can't believe you'd do that to my car. Watch your step, because I'm going to make it my mission to get you back," he teased.

"Why? You got the girl. You should be thanking me. Besides, Gramps thought it was genius."

"He knew?" Blake asked.

"Of course I knew." His grandfather had come up behind them, his timing impeccable. "Sarah tells me everything. Getting the two of you to figure out your feelings for one another hasn't been easy, but I'm glad it's finally happened. Now, I've got Blake back in town, a soon to be new granddaughter in the family, a great-grandson, and hopefully, another great-grandchild in short order. I hear the maternity leave at Peterson's is quite generous." He grinned, pulling Zoe in for a hug. "Good to see you again."

"You too," she offered, smiling at the older man. It felt like she was home, all of her favorite people around her.

"Grandpa, you're getting ahead of yourself. Give us some time to see where this is going. We haven't even officially dated yet."

Zoe nodded in agreement. It was a lot to take in all at once, and it would be best to rein in the wedding plans until they'd had more time together. "He's right. It's really too soon and we need time to make sure this will last. I've already made one mistake. This time I need to get it right. Forever."

"Forever sounds good to me." Blake kissed her right there in front of Sarah and his grandfather.

"Public display of affection, son? Thought I taught you better." Robert Peterson joined them, an odd look on his face.

"You taught me to love the right woman the way you loved Mom. That's what I'm doing," Blake said, unwilling to back down or let go of Zoe.

"Then I reckon you found the right woman, judging by your actions." And right then and there, Blake's dad grinned. The first she'd seen on his face in as long as she could remember.

"About time you came around," Mack exclaimed, clapping his son on the back.

Blake's father nodded. "Reckon so. Margie would have loved Zoe," he said, tears glistening in his eyes. He leaned forward, pulling Blake in for a man-to-man bear hug. "I'm sorry I've been so hard on you. After I lost your mother, I felt as though my joy was gone. I wanted to hold on to the past, afraid that new would wash away the memories I have. I was wrong to shut you out. And I hope you'll forgive an old fool set in his ways."

"Of course. I never understood your attitude, but now, I get it. Without Zoe, I'd be lost and doing the same thing, I'm afraid."

"We haven't even gone on a date yet. Do you mind if we don't start talking about losing each other?" Zoe said, pushing Blake playfully in the shoulder. The two men were finally settling their differences, and Zoe couldn't have been happier for them.

Epilogue

S IX MONTHS LATER…

Grandpa had gotten his wish. It only took Blake two weeks, five days, and three hours to know that forever was the only option for him and Zoe. She was his heart and soul, and life without her would be empty. It hadn't come as a surprise to anyone when they got engaged. The pastor of their church had been more than accommodating when it came to the arrangements, and they were married less than a month later.

It had surprised them, however, when his grandfather had given them the ice cream shop as a wedding present. For Zoe, it was a dream come true. For Blake, having Zoe by his side was *his* dream come true.

The first thing they'd done was take a week-long honeymoon. Just the two of them while Sarah stayed with Scott. The second week was family week—at Disney World.

His father had surprised them all with a family trip. Hotel. Flights. Admission tickets. Basically, an all-expenses-paid trip to Disney World. Scott had been overjoyed, especially when he discovered the plans included Great Grandpa Peterson, Grandpa Peterson, his Aunt Sarah, Zoe and Blake, *and* Devon.

It had been a blast watching the boys have a wonderful time. Hard to keep up with and exhausting, but overwhelmingly a great time. A memory. And soon, they'd have more memories.

Blake took Zoe's hand and brought it to his heart, placing his other hand on her belly. "How's Mommy doing today?" he asked.

"The morning nausea wasn't as bad. In fact, I think I'm craving some ice cream," Zoe said, smiling up at him. Her hair was pulled back in a ponytail, and he leaned forward to kiss the velvety skin of her neck.

"Little Susie Marie Peterson is going to be one spoiled child," he murmured. Zoe had agreed to name their baby girl after his mother and grandmother. In fact, it had been her idea. Her love knew no bounds, and Blake considered himself the luckiest man in the world to have her by his side.

"That tickles." Zoe laughed, rubbing her neck. "But why would you think she'll be spoiled?"

"Because her mother has a passion for ice cream, and she owns an ice cream shop. Doubly dangerous." Blake chuckled.

"There is that." Not to mention the amount of love they had overflowing was more than enough to envelope Scott and Susie. His family.

The dog nudged Zoe's hand, wanting to be included in the fun.

"Good boy, Hank. We both have reason to celebrate, don't we?" Blake reached out to pet the dog.

Woof Woof.

"See, he knows what I'm talking about. It's a guy thing." Blake patted the top of Hank's head and rubbed his side affectionately.

"I don't know if he understands about you, but the fact you're both becoming fathers is something to celebrate. I just wish baby Susie would be here as fast as the puppies will arrive," Zoe said, lavishing some love on the dog with him.

"All in good time, my love." Blake kissed his wife, leaning down to smooth Zoe's T-shirt across her belly and kiss the baby. They walked hand in hand toward the swing set where Hank had run back to keep an eye on Scott and Devon.

Life had taken several unexpected turns and they were all filled with love. It was like having his own personal Easter blessing that kept on giving and growing.

What to read next...

Love & Adventure
Book 9 of the Holidays in Hallbrook series – A Sweet Memorial Day/Father's Day Romance.
What do baseball and true love have in common besides a diamond? Is that a trick question?

If you enjoyed this sweet and charming romance, be sure to check out the

ALSO BY ELSIE DAVIS section on the next page for more clean and wholesome romance.

BONUS READ

Want to keep in touch with new releases and what's happening in the world of Elsie Davis?
Sign up for the monthly newsletter at Elsie Davis HEA (Happily-Ever-After) and enjoy DIGGING THE DRIVER (A Celebrity Corgi Romance) as a FREE BOOK!

The greatest compliment you could give an author is to leave a review in order to help other readers discover the same great stories you enjoyed. Amazon/Bookbub/Goodreads are all great places. Many thanks!!!
Another great way to keep in touch - *Follow Elsie Davis on FaceBook*

Also By Elsie Davis

Sweet, Clean and Wholesome Stories...with a Happily-Ever-After Guarantee!

Holidays in Hallbrook
(Sweet Romance Series for Holidays Throughout the Year)
Welcome to Hallbrook, New Hampshire. A small-town filled with the unexpected, lots of love, and of course, a beloved dog to ramp up the excitement.
Love & Order (Labor Day)
Love & Family (Thanksgiving)
Love & Peace (Christmas)
Love & Chocolate (Valentine's Day)
Love & Hope (Mother's Day)
Love & Liberty (Independence Day)
Love & Honor (Veteran's Day)

Love & Joy (Easter)
Love & Adventure (Father's Day)

Great Smoky Mountain Getaways
(Christian Inspirational – Women's Fiction Romances)
Juliet's Journey to Love
Poppy's Path to Love
Rachel's Road to Love

Crossroads Creek Cowboys
(Christian Inspirational Romances)
The Heart of a Cowboy
The Help of a Cowboy
The Return of a Cowboy
Coming Soon – The Care of a Cowboy

Crestfield Inn Romances
**If you like special kinds of soulmates, a splash of
the supernatural, and wholesome relationships,**

you'll adore this sweet bit of fun filled with ro-
mance and mystery.
Turning Back Time
Turning Up Roses
Turning Down Pie

Celebrity Corgi Romance
(Standalone Sweet Romance)
If you like light mystery mixed in with your hap-
pily-ever-after, you'll enjoy this second-chance
romance and the race to save an adorable Corgi.
Digging the Driver

Gold Coast Retrievers
(Sweet Romance)
**Special Golden Retrievers help their humans
solve mysteries, save lives, and even find love...**
Defending Dakota

Trinity River
(Sweet Western Romance)

Ranchers and farmers depend on the Trinity River for water, but when a secret conglomerate starts buying up property by fair means or foul, it's time for the landowners of Tumble County to fight back—Texas style. But what they don't count on, is finding love in the process.

Back in the Rancher's Arms

Small Town, Big Secrets

Coming Soon! (2023-2024)

Sundancer's Legacy – 9 Book series

Sundancer's Star

Sundancer's Joy

Sundancer's Heart

Sundancer's Majesty

Sundancer's Miracle

Sundancer's Glory

Sundancer's Kiss

Sundancer's Moon

Sundancer's Splendor

About The Author

Elsie Davis is a *USA Today and International Bestselling Author* of over 25 sweet, clean, and wholesome romances, and a member of the ACFW. She discovered the world of Happily-Ever-After romance at the age of twelve when she began avidly reading Barbara Cartland, the Queen of Romance, and has been hooked ever since. After building her dream log home on top of a small mountain, she turned her attention to do what she loves most, writing. Elsie writes sweet Contemporary Romance and Contemporary Christian Romance from her heart...hoping to share a little love in a big world.

When she's not writing, she can be found birding, kayaking, camping, fishing, playing disc golf, and taking nature walks—hoping to spot wildlife. Basically, she loves all things outdoors, EXCEPT cold weather. She and her husband are avid Caribbean cruisers, but Elsie's favorite vacation was their cruise to Alaska. (In spite of the cold!) Indoors, she enjoys a toasty fire, and of course, a great romance with a guaranteed Happily-Ever-After.

https://www.elsiedavishea.com